ABOUT THE AUTHOR

Ing____ ____ ____ ____ ____ ____ n
autl__ and jour_____ er books ha____ on numerous
awards and been translated into several languages. Her
fourth book, *Handgranateple*, was listed in the 2008
IBBY Honours List. She lives in Stockholm, Sweden.

Minus Me

INGELIN RØSSLAND

Translated by Deborah Dawkin

ROCK THE BOAT

A Rock the Boat Book

First published in North America, Great Britain & Australia by
Rock the Boat, an imprint of Oneworld Publications, 2015

Originally published in Norwegian as *Minus meg* by CAPPELEN DAMM in 2011

ISBN 978-1-78074-694-4
ISBN 978-1-78074-695-1 (ebook)

Typeset by Hewer Text UK Ltd, Edinburgh
Printed and bound in Great Britain by Clays Ltd, St Ives plc

This translation has been published with the financial support of NORLA.

Oneworld Publications
10 Bloomsbury Street
London WC1B 3SR
England

Stay up to date with the latest books,
special offers, and exclusive content from
Oneworld with our monthly newsletter

Sign up on our website
www.oneworld-publications.com

Minus Me

Chapter 1

The tram rattles along through the snowy streets. The window vibrates icily against Linda's forehead, stopping her from falling asleep. She tries pulling her woolly hat down between her face and the window, but it doesn't help. She sits up straight and looks out over the tram. It's almost empty. A teenage girl sits with her knees jammed up against the seat in front of her, purple tights showing through a rip in her jeans. She's using her scarf as a cushion to lean her head against the window. Linda doesn't have a scarf. But she's wearing a thick pair of orange mittens that her grandmother knitted for her. Extra big, so she'd have growing-room. Linda stretches her fingers. The middle one almost reaches the end now. She takes the mittens off, and is about to put them against the window, like the girl with the scarf, when a figure catches her eye. A boy, slightly older than Linda, is leaning against a lamp post. The whole of him, but especially his face, is softly but clearly lit. And he's gazing straight at her. It's as if he wants something. As if he's saying come here.

Just at that moment Linda feels a clamping sensation around her heart. She gasps for air, and just as the pain forces her to double up and close her eyes, she catches a last glimpse of the boy, running out into the road and towards the tram. There's a thud and the tram jolts on its way, and as it does the pain in her chest melts away as abruptly as it came. Her mittens tumble to the floor. One into a brownish pool of melted snow and grit. She's too weak to bend down for them. A scream rises inside her, but comes out like a silent breath. Her heart swells, then contracts, setting her blood in motion pounding round her ears.

What on earth happened? Linda looks around to see if anybody else has seen anything, but they obviously haven't. The girl nearer the front of the tram is still sitting as she was, knees tucked up, cheek resting against her scarf. The other passengers too are still rocking drowsily to the rhythm of the tram. Linda presses her face up to the window.

Where's the boy? What happened to the boy? Did he run into the side of the tram?

She gets up, grabs her sports bag and rushes to the back window to look. But there's nobody there, just the snow whirling up from the tramlines and the lights of a taxi following close behind. The taxi flashes to overtake, as the tram pulls up at a stop. Linda has to hold tight to prevent herself falling over. The doors open, sucking cold air into the tram. She feels a chill at the back of her neck. Turns. And there he is, standing right behind her. The boy. Eyes as blue as a husky's, frost on his long eyelashes melting and turning into pearls. The ceiling lights make tiny rainbows in the droplets.

She catches herself staring at him, looks down and bites her bottom lip.

'Are these yours?' asks the boy, holding out her orange mittens.

'How . . . ?'

'You'll still need them.'

She takes them. Shakes the one that fell into the muddy water.

She wants to thank him, but the words won't come out of her mouth. He answers her anyway:

'No problem,' he says.

He turns away from her to look out of the window and then presses the bell. Ducking to see under his arm, Linda realizes she's almost home.

'This is your stop,' he says, stepping aside for her.

'But how did you . . . ?'

'Shhhh . . .' he says, smiling with a finger to his lips. Again she feels the gust of cold wind from outside. She jumps out onto the pavement. She looks back to see if the boy is following her. But as the tram moves off, he's still standing there behind the closed doors.

Why had he spoken to her as though he knew her? As though he'd only got on the tram for her sake? Linda racks her brain, but can't recall ever having seen him before. Surely she would have remembered him; those intense eyes, the way he looked at her. Linda lifts her hand to wave to him. He shakes his head slowly but looks into her eyes, until the distance between them breaks their contact.

Linda breathes out. The white cloud that fills the air proves how cold it is. It's been minus twenty in the mornings recently.

She breathes in. The frosty air feels like a metal rasp in her lungs. Her heart tightens again, before setting into action once more, pumping warm blood round her body. Linda rolls the collar of her knitted pullover up over her mouth. It helps against the cold, but not the aching sensation she's had in her joints recently. She'd been relieved that Maria had arranged to meet her mum in town today, and couldn't walk home with her. Then Linda could sneak on the tram. Maria never has the guts to get on without paying. She's frightened that God can see her. Linda doesn't think God bothers himself over such details.

Chapter 2

The rambling old house where Linda lives is on the outskirts of Trondheim but it's only a few hundred metres from the tram stop. Linda walks between the school and St Elizabeth's Hospital before she turns into her street. She's surprised to see that the ground-floor light is on. The flat, where her grandmother used to live, has stood empty since she died last year. As Linda approaches she sees two figures moving around inside. Mum and Dad.

Her parents stop in the doorway, looking into the front room, which Granny used to call the library. Linda's father is standing behind her mother. He puts his arms around her waist and rests his chin on her shoulder, and then her mother leans her head back, lifts one arm and places her hand on his neck. She sees her father stroke her mother's stomach, and then slip his hand under her jumper. Linda takes a look around; imagine if a stranger or someone came along and saw. Her cheeks burn.

She takes off one of her mittens to fish her keys out of her pocket, and walks to the front door. She puts her key in the lock and gives it a tug; it's always extra stiff in the winter. Linda slips inside quickly and kicks the door to, giving it an extra shove with her shoulder to make sure it locks properly. Her mittens tumble to the floor in the hallway, and as she bends down to pick them up she can feel her heart distinctly. She remembers the boy, his gaze when he picked up her mittens, ice-cold, yet so intense and alive.

Was she feeling her heartbeat so clearly because she would soon be a teenager? Were boys beginning to give her weird feelings? They'd only ever irritated her before now. Axel, at least, only ever irritated her. He'd certainly never made her heart like this. But, then again, perhaps things would be different this summer. She'd be thirteen next time they saw each other. They'd both be teenagers. Perhaps Axel is online. It's a while since she heard from him. She almost misses his constant pestering. But why is she suddenly thinking about Axel? Linda looks at her watch, it's almost half past seven. She takes the stairs to the first floor in five long strides. Then she puts her key in the lock, only to find that the door is open.

The TV stands prattling to itself in one corner of the room, while the woodburner crackles in the other. Linda stretches out her fingers to get some warmth in them, then hurries to put her feet in the slippers that stand waiting for her by the woodburner. Looking down at her feet, she realizes her boots will never dry out there in the freezing cold hallway. Linda runs out into the hall, grabs them, and comes back in, shutting the door tight behind her. She goes over to woodburner and takes an old newspaper from the pile next to the log basket. She spreads it on the floor to stop the snow and dirt from her boots going onto the carpet. A headline catches her eye: GIRL DROPS DEAD AFTER HER FIRST KISS. Wow, that's so romantic, in a kind of sad and dramatic way, thinks Linda. The article is about a couple of kids in America. Further down it says that after the kiss, the girl sat down on the sofa in his flat, and that was where she died. Not from the kiss, but from a rare heart condition. Well, it was almost perfect, thinks Linda, putting her boots on the paper. Imagine if the girl had died in the boy's arms? That would have been far more romantic, if you were going to die at all.

Linda gets up to throw some more wood into the burner. The log basket is almost empty, so she decides to be helpful and fill it up. But first she wants to check if Axel is online. She grabs the tatty carrier bag from behind the log basket, and goes into her room. She flips her laptop open. The screen immediately springs to life, and with just a glimpse at the right-hand side, she sees he isn't there. She feels irritated at him again now. What can he be so busy with? Mia is online, however, and messages her. Linda bends forward to look at Mia's new profile picture then slams down the lid. What is it with Mia? Does Mia really think she'd waste her time on a brainless Barbie girl? As if! They hadn't been friends in the summer and she wasn't about to change that now.

Taking the shortcut through the apartment, she opens the door onto the backstairs.

Linda slips some clogs on before opening the door out to the little wooden bridge that crosses over the backyard to the outhouse. She holds the rail, since both the bridge and her clogs are slippery. On the other side of the bridge she lifts the latch on the outhouse door. A black cat streaks out from the darkness and runs down the steps into the backyard. It turns to look up at her, hissing quietly, before pissing on the corner of the house, and then leaping over the fence to disappear into the neighbour's backyard.

'What a nice guy,' mumbles Linda to herself, pressing the light switch just inside the door. She sniffs the air to see if the little beast has left its calling card in here too, but it hasn't. Linda fills the carrier bag with logs and hurries back into the flat. She hears her parents coming upstairs, and waits for the front door to open before tipping the logs into the basket.

'Ah, thank you, darling!' says her mother. 'That's wonderful.' Her voice is almost lost in the noise of the logs tumbling into the basket.

Linda tucks the bag back behind the woodburner. 'What were you doing in Granny's flat? I hope you're not thinking of having students down there too?'

'Not at all. We've got very different plans,' says her father grinning.

'Like what?'

'You'll find out soon enough.'

'Linda, have you been out with wet hair again?'

Linda's mother crosses the room and feels her hair. Linda pulls away.

'I've been wearing my woollen hat.'

'You must dry it properly before you go out in the snow, or you'll be ill,' says her mother in a worried voice, reaching out to touch her hair again. Linda dodges away.

'There was a queue at the hairdryer. If I had my own – one of those mini ones that fit in your sports bag – it would have been dry.'

'Are we off again? I want this and want that,' says her father.

'I didn't say I wanted a hairdryer. I was simply stating a fact.'

'Simply stating a fact, eh?' says her father, laughing.

'We'll see. It's your birthday soon. Thirteen!' says her mother. 'I remember when you were born. You lay in my arms, so pink and little. It was . . .'

'. . . love at first sight,' says her father, finishing her mother's sentence and putting his arm around her.

'Hmm . . . what is it with you two?' Linda snaps.

'What do you mean?' asks her mother.

'You're always hugging each other lately.'

'Isn't it good that we love each other?' asks her father.

'I suppose. Just don't carry on like that when my friends are round. It's weird. Okay?'

Her father lets go of her mother, and stretches his arms out to Linda. She knows what's next and lets out a squeal before he grabs her and swings her over his head.

'Careful with your back, Erik.'

'I'm as a strong as an ox and it takes nothing to throw this little thing up to the ceiling,' he answers.

Linda stretches and reaches out to touch the ceiling. As she does so, she sees a shadow out of the corner of her eye. There's a figure in the window of St Elizabeth's Hospital on the other side of the road. And like a flash, she knows it's the boy from the tram. She can feel his gaze and that weird sensation in her body again. Her fingers don't reach the ceiling, and instead she collapses onto her father's shoulder. Before she knows it, she's lying on the sofa by the woodburner.

'What did I say about that game, Erik? Linda's far too big for that now,' grumbles her mother.

'Are you alright, Linda?' says her father, stroking her cheek. 'You seem rather hot to me. You feel her, Ellen.'

Linda feels the touch of her mother's hand on her cheek, then her forehead, before hearing her worried voice saying Linda doesn't seem well. Her father lifts her up to take her into the bedroom.

'Do you want to lie in our bed?' he asks, hesitating at the doorway to her parents' room.

Linda shakes her head.

Her mother is a few steps ahead. She lifts the duvet to one side and tucks Linda in. Linda now has two pairs of worried eyes staring down at her. Whenever she's shown the least sign of getting ill, they've always wrapped her in cotton wool, taking time off work to make her warm milk and honey, or just to read aloud to her and stroke her hair. It's lovely, but you can have too much of a good thing. If Linda had siblings her parents would have had to share all this attention out between them. It's a bit much for one person to carry on their own. Linda sighs, and the lines on her parents' faces grow even deeper.

'I'm fine. I'm just a bit tired,' says Linda, smiling and trying to be reassuring.

Behind her parents, on the other side of the street, the shadow has moved to another window. Linda's smile freezes.

She feels sure the shadow is going to lift its hand and wave at her now, and she doesn't want to see it, so she closes her eyes.

'Can you switch the light off, please? I think I need to sleep a bit,' says Linda, with eyes tight shut.

'Let me help you off with your clothes, sweetie,' says her mother. Linda lets her. Layer after layer. Mummy's precious little doll.

Chapter 3

Linda is taking a shower. She woke up before everyone else, feeling completely better after yesterday's events. She probably just needed a proper night's sleep. Linda laughs at herself for this thought, it's so boringly grown-up. Linda turns up the temperature of the water, and stands there enjoying the steam as it fills the shower cabinet. But she listens out carefully for her parents, in case they wake up; they get cross when she uses too much hot water. She closes her eyes and feels the gushing water drum against her skin, and the warmth creep down over her stomach. Scenes from the summer roll across her mind; she sees herself fighting with Axel in the lake, she sees him stopping suddenly, his face close to hers, his hand reaching up to her cheek to brush away a strand of hair. She brings her own hand up to her cheek.

'Linda!'

There's a bang on the bathroom door and Linda turns off the water hurriedly.

'Yes!' she shouts.

She opens the shower door, grabs her bathrobe from the

hook and wraps herself in it before unbolting the bathroom door, almost stumbling on the slippery floor. Her mum rushes in, but instead of shouting at Linda, she apologizes and immediately crouches down in front of the lavatory.

'Aren't you well?' asks Linda, winding a towel like a turban round her head.

'Don't worry. It'll pass,' her mum groans. 'How are you feeling, darling?'

'I'm fine. Shall I boil some eggs?' asks Linda.

'Yes . . . do.'

Her mother retches.

'But just for you and Dad. I don't want any,' she says, waving her hand behind her.

Linda takes the hint and goes out into the kitchen, closing the door after her. She's seen it all before, her mother throwing up, the nervous but hopeful glances between her parents. Glances that say: will there be a baby this time? A little brother or sister for Linda? Another little one to love? But it's gone wrong each time. Her mother has lost two babies. The last a couple of years ago. Linda gets a lump in her stomach just thinking about it. It was in the summer, and they were at the cottage down in the south of Norway. She and Axel had borrowed a boat, without permission, and crashed it on some rocks, so it got a hole in the bottom. Everything turned out okay, they'd been rescued by some local fishermen, but they'd got a terrible telling-off. And that night, it happened. Her mother had started bleeding and her parents rushed to the hospital. They'd stopped talking about having more children after that.

Is that why they haven't said anything, Linda wonders, as she boils the eggs and puts on the coffee. Surely her parents can't believe she hasn't guessed? When she was little, Linda longed for a little brother or sister. But now . . . does she still? A screaming baby for whom she'll be expected to babysit and change nappies? What is she going to say to all her friends when her mum starts getting big? After all, her parents are getting on a bit; they're well over forty.

The eggs are ready. Looking in the saucepan she realizes she's boiled three after all. She sighs, rinses them under cold water and puts them in the eggcups on the table. While she's waiting for her parents to come to breakfast, she makes packed lunches for all three of them. It's never a bad idea to make an extra effort when it's your birthday soon – or if your mother is pregnant again.

'So you made eggs for everyone, after all?' says her mother, coming in from the bathroom. She's dressed now and has put her make-up on, but she still looks rather pale.

'Sorry, I did it without thinking. But there is bread, ham and jam also, if you prefer that.'

'That's okay. I'm feeling better now, so I'll try to eat a bit,' she says, ruffling Linda's hair as she takes off her turban. 'Shall I comb your hair for you afterwards?'

'I can manage, thanks. Are you ill or something, Mum?'

'For wanting to comb your hair?'

'No. You were being sick.'

'Oh, that . . . that's nothing to worry about. It's probably something I ate.'

Her mum folds the towel and puts it on the edge of the kitchen bench. Linda follows her movements, but doesn't ask if she's pregnant. She'll have to wait to be told.

'Erik!' her mother calls out. 'Are you finished in the bathroom? Linda's made breakfast.'

Linda's father comes out of the bathroom, hair wet and lips pursed ready to plant a kiss on her mother's cheek.

'Good morning, Mrs Larsen!' he says, laughing. 'Aren't we lucky to have such a grown-up daughter?'

'Oh, pur-lease!' says Linda, rolling her eyes.

'Oh, pur-lease!' imitates Linda's father, laughing. He pulls her over and gives her a hug. 'Now, let's eat.'

The extra time they'd gained by Linda getting up early and making breakfast is soon lost to eating their eggs. Her father looks at the clock and starts putting the milk and juice back in the fridge.

'Are you two coming to the diving competition tomorrow?' asks Linda, putting the packed lunch she's made into her bag.

'Are you sure you're well enough? You seemed so poorly yesterday,' says her mother.

'You're the one who's throwing up,' says Linda, getting annoyed by her mother's anxiety.

'We'll be there, alright. We want to see you win the whole caboodle!' her father interrupts with a grin.

This is an obvious attempt to stop any argument – or discussion. They never argue in this family, they discuss things. But today Dad doesn't want to do either. He collects the rest of the food on the table to put it back into the fridge, still with that ridiculous smile on his lips. Linda gets the urge to say something spiteful, but contents herself with being grouchy.

'Hmm, so you're thinking I'll win, eh?' she says, heading for the bathroom to brush her teeth.

'It's bound to be your turn some day!' says her mother, smiling. She hasn't touched her egg or even her coffee.

'That's not how it works. To win, you have to be the best,' says Linda.

'Hey! Look! We've got a visitor on the bridge.'

Dad takes Linda's arm and pulls her gently over to the window that overlooks the backyard. It's the cat from yesterday. Big and black, just sitting there and staring up at the window.

'Perhaps it's hoping to get a little titbit?' says her mother, who has joined them at the window.

'We'll never get rid of it then,' says Linda's father.

'I saw that cat yesterday too. It was in the outhouse when I went to get the logs.'

'How did it get in there?' her father says, surprised.

'Oh, you know what cats are like,' says her mother. 'It can have the rest of my sandwich.'

'Oh, Ellen, do you really want a cat hanging around just now?'

'A little slice of bread is not going to do any harm. And it probably belongs to someone else anyway. It's only visiting us.'

Linda's mother leans forward to open the window. The cat instantly gets up, and arches its back.

'Nice pussycat. Do you want some bread?'

The cat hisses back. Then just as it had the evening before, it walks down the steps into the backyard and stops to wee on the corner, before disappearing over the neighbour's fence.

'Seems like you'll have to eat your breakfast yourself,' says Linda's father, laughing and closing the window. 'Brrr, it's cold. Isn't spring ever going to come?'

'February isn't exactly spring,' her mother replies.

'Where I come from, spring begins in February,' he says.

'You're over-romanticizing. And you should be used to Trondheim seasons by now. And we're not going down to the south coast this Easter, Erik. We're going up to the cabin in the mountains.'

'When will you understand that Easter is the time for boat-mending and bonfires by the fjord?'

'And when will you realize that all good Norwegians go skiing at Easter?'

'Not us from the South.'

'Oh, yes. Even you from the South. Think of all those people from the South who have won Olympic medals for skiing.'

'But I want to go to the South too,' says Linda.

'We agreed to go every other year. Now, off you go and brush your teeth,' says her mother.

Linda goes obediently into the bathroom. She squeezes a generous dollop of toothpaste onto her brush. She looks over at the shower. A warm tummy, burning cheeks. She brings her hand up to her face and tucks a lock of hair behind her ear. Slowly and gently, just like Axel did in the summer. His breath felt so close. What an idiot he is. Linda ruffles her hair out again. It's wet. She'll have to blow-dry it before she goes.

Chapter 4

The snow floats down silently outside the windows of the swimming hall, each snowflake becoming one with the sea. Not a single flake will be lost. From cloud to air to sea and back again to air and cloud. Nothing is ever lost. Inside the hall, on this side of the windows, there is water, steam, chlorine, crowds, warm breath, and Linda standing at the very top of the diving tower. Her moment has come. She looks out over the swimming hall, at all the people in the stands. At her mum and dad. They are smiling, but they don't dare wave for fear of distracting her before her dive. The dive that's going to be perfect; that has to be perfect if she's ever going to have her turn at winning 'the whole caboodle', as Dad puts it. She can see Maria down there too. Maria with her bright-red towel draped over her shoulders like a victory cape. It seems in keeping. Maria has won everything. Maria always wins 'the whole caboodle'. She is smiling at Linda now and giving her the thumbs-up. It's easy, thinks Linda, to be generous to someone who doesn't pose any threat, who barely counts as competition.

Shifting her weight from her right foot to her left, Linda glances round the swimming hall once more. The air is filled with expectation. Her gaze stops at a pair of polar-blue eyes. It's the boy from the tram. He's looking straight up at her. Suddenly she feels her heartbeat slow down, and her chest rise and fall calmly. All sound melts away. Her concentration gathers. Her muscles are poised. She knows what she has to do now. In her mind she runs through every moment of the dive ahead. She knows this one is going to be perfect. And even though she loses eye contact with the boy as she jumps, she can still feel his gaze, and senses it calming her nerves. And as she descends towards to the water she feels she has all the time in the world: time to realign her body perfectly after her somersault; time before she breaks through the glassy surface of the pool, without a sound, without a ripple. And as soon as she is under the water, Linda is already smiling, sure of what awaits her the moment she surfaces. She pops up at the side of the pool, takes a deep breath and wipes the water from her face. She is greeted by the sound of clapping from the stands. Her parents are on their feet. They're no longer afraid to wave, and her mother can't stop jumping up and down. Linda jumps and pulls herself out of the water. Maria is there in an instant, hugging her. Now they are both wrapped in the red victory cape. They look up at the scoreboard and as the final scores appear, what everyone thought is confirmed: Linda is in the lead. Maria gives her a kiss on the cheek.

'Wow, you rock, Linda!' says Maria, giving her a hug. 'That was amazing!' Linda looks at her friend. She seems genuinely happy for her. How can Maria always be so nice? So happy for others, even if it means letting someone else take the glory?

'I've no idea how it happened,' says Linda, wriggling from her friend's embrace and picking up her own towel. How often has she watched Maria do brilliantly, and felt a pang of jealousy rather than genuine pleasure?

'Excellent, Miss Larsen,' says her coach. 'That was very good indeed. Why can't you always concentrate like that, hmm?'

He sounds pleased, even though his tone is rather brusque.

'I don't know,' says Linda, with a shrug. She lets her gaze roam over the crowd for a glimpse of the boy. Was he actually there? Linda feels a weird tingling sensation in her body and suddenly dark spots appear in front of her eyes. Maria grabs her by the arm.

'Are you okay, Linda?' Maria asks.

'Yeah, sure,' she replies, straightening up.

'You looked like you were about to faint,' says Maria, giving her a concerned rub with the towel.

'A bit giddy, that's all.'

'Here, have this banana and plenty to drink in the break,' says her coach, before giving her a pat on the back.

Linda sees a new expression in his face, a sort of pride – or is it hope? She smiles back, suddenly aware of not wanting to disappoint him. She determines to make her next dive equally good. For the first time ever she feels she could actually win.

'Visualize your next dive during the break, Miss Larsen. This is set to be a great competition for us, girls,' says the coach, clapping his hands three times to emphasize the significance of what he's said. As the two friends wander back to the changing rooms Maria gives Linda a poke in the side, and mimics him: 'Visualize your next dive in the break, girls. Imagine you're a banana, girls. Enter the water like a silent tiger!'

Hanging back for a moment, Linda casts her eye over the stands again. Maybe the boy hadn't been there at all. Had she been mistaken? She gets her answer with a bump.

'Congratulations!'

'What?'

'Impressive dive,' says the boy, standing in front of her. It's warm here in the swimming hall, and yet he's still wearing the same coat he had on in the tram. He has a pale face with dark circles under his eyes and a bluish tint around his mouth.

'Thank you,' says Linda, looking at him. She's about to say more and to ask him who he is, but he quickly bows and leaves. What sort of boy goes around bowing to girls? Nobody in her class, that's for sure. She watches him leave, his coat flapping behind him. What is with that coat? And the make-up? He must be wearing mascara on those eyelashes.

'Hey, Linda, are you coming?' says Maria, poking her head round the changing-room door.

'Yes, stop nagging!'

Linda wraps her towel more closely around her and hurries into the changing room after her friend.

Chapter 5

Linda sits down on a changing-room bench and leans against the wall.

'Are you going to eat that banana, or just sit there hugging it?'

'Eat it, I suppose.'

Linda peels the banana, divides it into two and gives half to Maria before chucking the peel in the bin.

'Are you alright?' asks Maria, with a mouthful of banana.

'Yes, but . . . well I felt kind of odd.'

'How do you mean?'

'When I was diving. It didn't feel like it was me doing it. I always feel kind of nervous beforehand, but this time I felt totally calm,' Linda explains.

'If our coach could hear you now he'd be overjoyed!'

'There was this boy looking up at me when I was on the diving board. He had such an intense look in his eyes, and then he nodded at me and I felt so calm and focused.'

'Was he good-looking?'

'Didn't you see him? He bumped into me just now, outside the changing rooms.'

'No, I didn't notice. You'll have to point him out to me afterwards.'

'I think he left.' Linda looks down at the piece of banana in her hand. She feels nauseous and wants to throw it away.

'While we're on the subject of boys, I've got something for you. Markus gave me a letter to give to you. It's from Oscar.'

Maria takes an envelope out of the side pocket of her bag. She waves it in front of her nose, sniffing it demonstratively.

'Mmm, perfume! A love letter, perhaps?' suggests Maria, winking before holding the letter under Linda's nose. Linda pulls back, another wave of nausea coming over her.

'Yuck! Has he smothered it in his mum's perfume – or his granny's?'

'Don't be so negative, Linda. You've got a perfumed love letter. Now, open it!'

Linda does and fishes out a sheet of paper decorated with stickers of dogs, flowers and kittens. No doubt stolen from his little sister, thinks Linda, before reading:

To Linda!
    You are one of the coolest people I know and also really CUTE (did you know Linda means 'beautiful' in Spanish?)! I could be your boyfriend if you like.
    Your very own (if you want, that is),
    Oscar.

Maria grabs the letter and reads it aloud before handing it back to Linda.

'You have got to say yes!'

'Have I?'

'Yes! Oscar is Markus's best friend. It's perfect! We can go on double dates! And tonight we can go to the cinema to celebrate!'

'Celebrate what?'

'Your amazing dive and the fact you've got a new boyfriend!' says Maria.

'I'm not sure . . .'

'But he's the second best-looking boy in school.'

'Well, okay – but shouldn't I be in love first?'

'Are you thinking about that Axel guy again?'

'No. Axel's an idiot.'

'You're in love with Axel, that's why you think he's an idiot. It's just like in *Anne of Green Gables* – one minute she hates that guy Gilbert, and the next minute she loves him. You don't have a clue sometimes.'

'Well, if you're right, then I can't go out with Oscar.'

'You what? Axel lives in Stavanger and Oscar lives in Trondheim.'

'He doesn't live in Stavanger, he lives further south than that.'

'Ugh, it's all the same. The point is that it's better to have a boyfriend that lives in the same city. Then you can get a bit of experience.'

'What do you mean?'

'If you go out with Oscar, then you'll have to kiss him. I mean; you haven't actually kissed anyone yet, have you?'

Maria sighs and goes over to the mirror to tidy her wet

hair. She tightens her ponytail and stands on tiptoe so she can see more of herself. Running her fingers under the edges of her red swimsuit, she straightens it at the tops of her thighs. Her legs are the colour of milky chocolate. Linda gazes at her friend's reflection. She's got small breasts under her swimsuit now too. They weren't there in the autumn.

Linda looks down at herself, at her skinny, milk-white legs. It's hardly surprising she's never been kissed. But she certainly seems to catching the boy-bug or something. Is Maria right? Is she actually in love with Axel? Again she thinks of last summer. She sees the sun flashing in the water. An inflatable blue mattress viewed from below. Her hands tipping the mattress over. A body rolling into the water. Hands reaching out. Axel's hand grabbing her ankle. The surface of the water rushing towards her. Axel's head popping up beside hers. His face close to hers. His hand tucking a strand of hair behind her ear. His lips moving: You're like a dolphin.

'Wakey-wakey! You're dreamy today,' says Maria.

'I'm sorry, Maria.'

'We should get back out there now.'

Maria turns to leave without waiting. Linda gets up, but feels faint. She steadies herself and manages to stay on her feet. Linda is relieved to see that Maria has walked on oblivious.

'You should give Oscar some serious thought,' Maria says, looking back over her shoulder. 'You don't want to end up like my big sister, do you?'

'What's wrong with her?'

'Sixteen and never been kissed!'

Chapter 6

Markus and Oscar come down from the stands. As usual,
Oscar walks a couple of steps behind Markus, wearing slightly
baggier trousers and shuffling his feet more than his friend.
Maria goes to meet the boys. She also walks a little ahead,
with her towel still draped over her shoulders like a cape,
more for effect than to actually cover herself. Markus takes
Maria's hand. Linda sees him squeeze it, and then sees Maria
squeeze his. Then he kisses Maria on the cheek, and she
giggles, pushing him away as if she's shocked. But it's clear
that she likes it, so much so that she kisses him back. Maria
kisses the best-looking boy in school. And just behind him
stands (according to Maria, at least), the second best-looking
boy. The boy who has written a perfumed love letter to Linda.
The boy who probably wishes he had a fringe covering his
face right now, but who has hair that sticks right up, giving
him nowhere to hide. Linda hasn't got anywhere to hide,
either, however hard she tries to stand behind Maria or stare
at the floor tiles.

'That was a great dive,' says Oscar.

'Thanks,' says Linda. 'And thanks for the letter.'

'Letter' is the magic word that tears Maria and Markus from each other. They turn to Linda and Oscar excitedly. Oscar looks down and shoves his hands in his pockets. If they'd been outside he'd have kicked at the gravel with his shoe, but there are only smooth tiles. Maria gives her a gentle nudge. Linda looks up at him.

'Okay. I'll be your girlfriend.'

'You will?'

The sunlight hits Oscar's face. Perhaps red hair isn't that bad after all, thinks Linda. Oscar takes a step towards her and she instantly feels her mouth go dry. Surely he's not going to kiss her? But no, he's not; he just pats her arm. Her arm is completely white, but still browner than his, even though he's covered in freckles. His hands are freckled too.

'Congratulations!' says Markus.

'Yes, congratulations, both of you!' says Maria. 'How about the four of us go and see a film together tonight?'

'The boys get to pick the film!' says Markus.

'I don't think so! Linda's in first place on the scoreboard and I'm in second. So it's girls' night tonight. Isn't that right, Linda?'

'Yeah, sure,' says Linda, less than thrilled at having a new boyfriend and a double date.

'Well, Oscar?' says Maria.

'Sounds fair to me,' Oscar replies.

'Oh my God, Oscar!' protests Markus. 'Ten seconds with a woman and you're already a doormat.'

'We ought to go,' says Linda, dragging Maria off.

She can't stand Oscar mauling her arm any more. It makes her feel totally naked. She doesn't even glance back at him, as they head off to join their team mates.

'Everything alright, Miss Larsen?' asks the coach as they return. Linda nods and sits down on the bench.

'Good. I hope you didn't spend your entire break talking to boys, girls. Mental preparation and focus are half the dive. More, actually.'

Maria pulls a face.

'I saw that, Yustino.'

Maria flashes him a sweet smile, then throws off her towel in preparation for her next dive. Linda stays behind on the bench. She looks over to where the boys are sitting, but instantly regrets it when she sees Oscar staring over at her and waving enthusiastically. Linda gives a tiny wave back, and then puts both hands very firmly in her lap.

She turns to look at Maria on the diving board. But again her mind drifts off. She is transported to a summer's day down on the south coast. She and Axel are lying on their backs in the grass, gazing up at the sky with pieces of straw in their mouths. She can feel the thin straw tickling her cheek. She scratches. Axel is propped up on his elbows. He smiles and Linda can see his slightly wonky tooth.

'I've missed you,' says Axel.

The moment is shattered by the voice of girl.

'Why didn't you wait for me?'

It's Mia, desperately out of breath. Mia in the stupid pink dress that barely covers her summer-brown skin, with hair so blonde it's practically white, and the sun glinting on dental braces in her stupid gawping mouth.

Linda shuts her eyes and shakes her head, trying to wipe the image of Mia from her retina. She opens her eyes again, and tries to bring her focus back onto Maria's dive. Maria is flying through the air, and after a perfect somersault she breaks the surface of the water like a silent missile, before surfacing immediately at the edge of the pool. She smiles. A smile that gets even broader when she sees the results board.

'Bravo, Yustino! If you keep this up on the last two dives, you'll have it in the bag!' shouts the coach, clapping his hands. 'That's if Miss Larsen doesn't beat you with her next dive,' he adds in a quiet voice, looking over at Linda.

Linda tries to smile back, but can't bring herself to. She feels sure the coach has already lost faith in her. It's written all over his face that he thinks Linda's super-dive was a fluke, and if she's honest, she feels the same. Who is she kidding? Does she really think she's going to win a medal or something?

Chapter 7

Linda's foot slips on the first step, but she regains her balance. She sees Maria has an anxious look on her face, so she smiles at her and waves. Then she looks over at her parents, who are smiling and waving enthusiastically at her, and then further towards Oscar who gives her two thumbs-up. He's my boyfriend now, she thinks. It's so strange. Even stranger if Maria's right about her being in love with that idiot Axel. If that's true, then being Oscar's girlfriend is all wrong. It's lucky there'll be so many tomorrows, so she can untangle this mess. Maybe she should break it off with Oscar tonight? But what should she say? Sorry, Oscar, I've changed my mind? Just the thought of it makes her stomach churn.

She closes her eyes and takes a deep breath. When she opens them again she sees the coach sitting down there on the bench. He has told them to think about their dives and not about boys. He looks up at her, and Linda looks out at the stands, even though she knows it will make her even more nervous. The seat where the boy was sitting before is empty. It's hardly surprising since she saw him leave. But she continues to scan the crowd until she finally spots him. He's sitting further away this time, on the bottom row. He is blowing into his hands as if he is cold. His gaze is fixed on her. Linda feels goosebumps rising on her arms. The boy nods at her again, but this time her heart refuses to steady. Instead it feels as though it were stuttering. As though it were coughing and spluttering like a worn-out car engine.

Linda hesitates, feels the diving board beneath her feet. She's reluctant to cast herself out into this precisely planned dive. The boy nods at her. But the soles of her feet are glued to the board. He nods again. Hesitantly she lifts one foot. Then she jumps, even though her heart is stuttering so unevenly. Dunk, de-de-dunk, dunk, de, dunk. As Linda enters the surface of the water, her heart stops stuttering. There's complete silence. Linda is under the water. Everything is utterly silent. And she is sinking. Sinking to the bottom of the pool. Then suddenly her body pops to the surface like a cork, with her back turned upwards, and the rest of her body drooping down into the water. She looks like a four-legged creature with a bowed head.

And above her limp body, the silence is filled with loud screams.

'Call an ambulance! For God's sake, call an ambulance!' cries the coach, before leaping into the pool. He grabs Linda, turns her over, and lifts her face above the water. Holding her head, he swims on his back towards the edge and then pulls her out onto the cold tiles. Quickly and decisively, he is following all the procedures they were taught in their lifesaving classes.

Linda is lying flat on her back at the edge of the pool. But a part of her has stepped out of her body, and is floating up so she can see what's happening. She looks down at the pale body in the red swimsuit, and watches the coach bend over her. In slow motion, Linda watches the droplets fall from the coach's wet hair onto her chest, as he tries to pump her heart into action. He leans over her mouth, breathes into her, watches her ribcage rise, breathes into her again, and again watches her ribcage. Then he places his hands on her chest again, and pumps hard. Linda remembers how she'd always thought it looked really brutal when this was demonstrated on the first-aid doll, but she can feel nothing now. And the sounds have melted away too. Or have they just been swapped for another sound? A soft droning sound. Or a gentle humming. She's never heard anything like it before. But it's a good sound, a safe sound. And strangely enough she doesn't feel afraid.

Linda sees her parents rush over. Her mother's lips are moving, but there's no sound coming out. Or perhaps Linda just can't hear what she's saying? Her mother falls to her knees and takes hold of one of Linda's limp hands. Meanwhile, her father kneels down behind her mother, and holds her shoulders so tight his knuckles turn white. Her mother's lips move again, but this time Linda knows she must have said something, because her father clearly replies, as he crouches there, stroking her with both hands.

Then something happens. With his winter coat flapping behind him like a cape, he comes striding along the edge of the pool; the boy with eyes like a husky dog. He stops at

Linda's feet and lifts his gaze upwards. Up to the Linda who is floating above the drama that is unfolding down at the poolside. Is she visible, then? Linda stretches her hand out in front of her. Yes, she can see her hand, just as clearly as the body that's lying below her. Wow! She wants to wave and to shout out that she's here, tell them that they can all relax. Then she catches sight of the body below her again, and notices that the lips have started to turn blue. What's happening? Is she dying? That's not possible! She can't just die like this, without a fight! Linda thrashes about with her arms, trying to descend to her body. The boy, who up until now has just been standing there watching her, suddenly nods and kneels down beside her body. The coach has turned away with his face hidden in his hands. Linda struggles to come down; it's as though she's too light. Then she sees the boy's fist come crashing down into her chest. In a violent swirl, like water when you pull out the plug, she comes down towards her body at the pool's edge. Thank you, God, she thinks, before she is suddenly blinded by a bright light like the flash of a camera.

Chapter 8

The wheelchair rolls down the corridor, its wheels going round and round, eating up the floor. Linda is freezing cold, but can't be bothered to ask for the blanket that her father is carrying with her mother's handbag. Her mother is pushing the chair, the rubber soles of her shoes squeaking against the linoleum floor. Linda's heart stutters in her chest; it doesn't beat properly, it just stutters.

A fourth tube is filled with blood, and the nurse asks Linda if she is okay. Linda can't be bothered to answer; it seems such a stupid question. Her mother is holding her hand, squeezing it too hard and smiling too much. Her father is standing over by the door. His hair looks like limp grass. The nurse attaches a fifth tube to the syringe, and places tube number four into something that reminds Linda of a see-saw. The blood sloshes back and forth in the tubes. Linda thinks the room has a metallic smell.

'Just one more now, and it's over,' the nurse tells her, holding tube number six at the ready.

'My little superhero,' says Linda's mother, tears welling up in her eyes. But despite her tears she keeps on smiling at

Linda. That ever-hopeful, encouraging smile. That 'everything will be alright' smile. Her father tries to smile too, but he's not as well-practised at faking it.

And then the wheels go round and round again, and her heart stutters and splutters, and they're off to another room. The corridor smells as you'd expect a hospital corridor to smell; a mixture of soap, plastic and pee. Linda is too tired to feel frightened, too absorbed in feeling her heart. She can barely take in anything that happens in this last room. But she sees the doctor holding up a picture of a heart. He tells them that it's her heart, and points at it with his ballpoint pen.

'Can her heart get better on its own?' asks her mum, looking at the vague grey shadows on the X-ray, which apparently represent her heart.

'I'm afraid all we can hope is that a suitable donor comes up in time.'

Linda looks over at her mother.

'That someone gives you their heart, Linda, darling.'

'But surely people need their hearts themselves,' Linda says sadly.

The doctor doesn't reply. He just puts the X-ray into a brown envelope.

'Sometimes there's a traffic accident or something, which means that somebody dies and can donate their heart to someone else,' her mother explains.

'So I have to hope somebody else has an accident? Is that it?'

'I have to be honest; even if we find a suitable donor in time, the chances are minimal,' says the doctor, looking away.

'Am I going to die?' asks Linda, shocked at the calmness of his voice.

'You have a rare heart condition. Actually it's a miracle that you survived this episode. It was lucky there were so many people at the swimming pool when it happened, so you were brought back to life,' says the doctor, fidgeting with the envelope.

Linda feels laughter building up inside her. She remembers the newspaper article about the girl who died after her first kiss. And now this has happened to her. The difference being that she was brought back to life. Plus, that she's never been kissed.

'What is it?' asks her mother.

Linda suddenly realizes she's laughing out loud, and that she's not managed to hold back.

The doctor puts the envelope in Linda's lap.

'Is there absolutely nothing you can do?'

'There's not a lot I can recommend, apart from taking it completely easy. Linda mustn't do anything to exert herself. No more sports, and that includes diving.'

'And if I don't take it easy?' says Linda, not quite sure how she's finding the energy to challenge him.

'Well, that could result in fatality,' he answers.

'Result in fatality?' asks Linda, unable to hide her irritation at the doctor's pompous language.

'Well, we . . . er . . . we don't know what your heart can withstand,' the doctor says hesitantly.

'So I'm going to die anyway?'

The doctor clicks his ballpoint pen before returning it to the breast pocket of his white coat.

'You've cheated death once, so there's absolutely no reason to give up hope,' says the doctor, walking towards the door. 'Thank you for coming, Linda. I look forward to seeing you again.'

And suddenly they're back on the ward. Linda is lying in bed, pretending to be asleep. She doesn't want to look at her mother, who is standing by the window with that over-optimistic smile on her face. Nor can she bear to look at her father, who is incapable of disguising his fear. His hands are constantly moving, as though they want to grab hold of something. But there is nothing to grab hold of now; they have been given absolutely no hope. Just a mangled heart in a brown envelope.

'Look! Do you see that black cat?' says Linda's mother.

'Where?' says her father.

'There. Isn't it the same one that we saw back at home?'

'Oh, Ellen, the town's full of black cats.'

'But it can't be a coincidence.'

'I'd say that's exactly what it is,' he answers. 'A coincidence.'

Chapter 9

With plaits dangling from under a woolly hat like two bits of rope, the girl runs towards the crossing. She shouts something and waves to some girls on the other side of the street. The girls turn and wave back. She runs out into the road without looking. There's a screeching of brakes. The body of the girl lies crushed on the asphalt.

'Wakey-wakey, Linda. It's your turn.' Maria shakes her gently by the arm.

'Ah, yes,' says Linda, screwing up her eyes and shaking her head to chase away the awful daydreams that keep coming back. Children she imagines mown down by buses, trailers, trains or charging bulls. All the dead children who are her only hope, she thinks, with a metallic taste in her mouth.

She opens her eyes, throws the dice and moves one of her Ludo counters.

'What were you thinking about just now?' Maria asks.

Linda refuses to answer, but hands the dice to Maria.

Maria throws and moves a counter.

'What are you thinking about?' Linda asks.

Angrily she grabs Maria's counter and moves it back to where it was, then takes another of Maria's counters and moves it so it knocks three of her own off the board.

'What's happening?' says Maria.

'Can't you see?' says Linda. 'You're winning and I'm losing.'

'I meant with you?'

'Please, can't we just play this game?'

'You're the best friend I've ever had. I don't want you to die. You're not allowed to die.'

Linda wishes Maria wouldn't keep whinging on; it's like a rodent gnawing at her stomach. As if whining will help. It just makes things worse. It makes her feel like it's her fault she's lying in a hospital bed. It makes her feel that she should have done something differently. But things are as they are. Linda wants to scream and chuck the dice and all the counters into Maria's face. But she doesn't. She picks up the dice calmly and passes them to Maria, who weighs them in her hand, then suddenly puts them down and gets up from her chair.

'Now what's the matter?' says Linda, sighing.

'I just need the toilet,' says Maria, unable to hide the tears in her voice. 'Anyway, it's your go.'

'Could you bring me some water?' asks Linda, taking a glass from the bedside table and giving it to her friend.

'Sure. Do you need anything else?'

'Yes . . . stop letting me win at Ludo.'

Maria takes the glass and goes. Linda sits there in her bed. She starts to tidy the game away. One of the counters falls to the floor and rolls under the bed. Linda swings her feet out onto the floor, but tries to get up too quickly. The world starts to spin. And as she hits the floor she is sucked back into another room and another time. A time when she and Maria could just have fun together. A time when Maria didn't cheat so Linda would win at Ludo or whisper tearfully that Linda mustn't die. A time that seems so far away now, even though it's been only a week.

Linda remembers lying on her bed with Maria, their feet resting up against the wall.

'I've decided to start wearing make-up,' says Maria, looking at her friend.

'Why?' says Linda, turning to face her.

'Because I'm nearly thirteen! We're going to be teenagers soon. Think of all the experiences we'll have!'

'Like what?'

'Kissing boys!'

'Yeah, but you started kissing them when you were four. And you and Markus are always kissing and cuddling.'

'But when you're a teenager you kiss more passionately, out of love and things.'

'Oh, Maria!' Linda rolls her eyes. She can't see why everything should change just because you're thirteen. It's only a number!

'Well?' says Maria, rolling onto her side to face Linda. Maria looks so happy. And so pretty, too. Perfect Maria. She won't have any problems being a teenager. She probably won't even get spots.

'You're completely boy-mad,' says Linda.

'You bet! And we've got to go to parties.'

'The world's coolest parties,' says Linda, getting drawn into her friend's excitement despite herself.

'And slow dance.'

'And get periods,' says Linda, mostly because she knows that Maria hates blood so much it makes her faint.

'Linda!'

'Okay, then. Go on language exchanges.'

'Go on holiday without our parents.'

'Go to college in America,' suggests Linda.

'I'll be a cheerleader!' says Maria, waving her arms.

'And I can be President!'

'No, you can't.'

'I can!'

'Say something sensible.'

'I'm not sure if I really want to be a teenager!' Linda admits, biting her nails. 'It all seems so – I don't know – so difficult.'

Maria suddenly sits up on the bed, looking extremely serious, and takes Linda's hands in hers.

'There is one very, very important thing, Linda.'

'What's that?'

'You have got to stop biting your nails,' says Maria, keeping a straight face for a second before bursting into laughter, throwing herself over Linda and tickling her. Linda tickles Maria back, and they roll onto the floor howling with laughter and gasping for breath. The door opens and Linda's mother peeps in.

'What on earth are you doing?'

'We're talking very seriously about the future,' Linda replies.

Her mother just shakes her head, before closing the door and leaving the girls to themselves again.

'Linda?' says Maria, taking her hand. 'We've got to make a list.'

'What sort of list?' wonders Linda.

'A list of all the things we've got to do when we're thirteen,' answers Maria.

Chapter 10

Maria comes back into the hospital room. Linda hears the glass of water tumble onto the floor, and feels a splash of water on her cheek. She can't be bothered to open her eyes. She just wants to go on sleeping here on the floor.

'Linda! Linda! Wake up!'

Maria crouches down next to her and pulls her up onto her lap. Linda opens her eyes.

'Hi.'

Maria hugs her in reply.

'Your mascara's running,' says Linda, looking up at her friend.

'I don't want you to die,' says Maria, hugging Linda even tighter.

'Do you remember that list we wrote?'

Linda lifts a hand and wipes away the mascara from under Maria's eyes with the sleeve of her nightdress.

'What list?'

'The list of all the things we were going to do when we were thirteen,' answers Linda.

'What about it?'

'It just popped into my head.'

'Oh?'

'If I die, will you promise to complete it?'

'But you're not going to die!' Maria shouts. Linda is suddenly aware of how hard her friend is squeezing her. And she can smell that she is wearing perfume. Maria smells of flowers in a garden in July.

'Will you promise?' says Linda.

'We're going to do everything on that list together.'

'I don't think so,' says Linda, closing her eyes.

Maria hugs her again, but Linda keeps her eyes closed.

'If you leave me, that list won't mean a thing.'

Linda doesn't answer, but she opens her eyes and lets Maria help her get back onto her feet and into bed. Linda lies under the duvet. She folds her hands over her chest, and shuts her eyes again. Then she says, quite matter-of-factly, she doesn't want carnations at her funeral.

'I hate carnations,' she says.

'I hate you talking about dying.'

'But I'm going to die, so we might as well talk about it. Will you sing for me, at the funeral?' asks Linda.

'Linda, I'll go if you don't shut up,' says Maria, stepping back from the bed.

'You can sing that one – "My Heart Will Go On". You know – from that film we saw about the boat that was meant to be unsinkable, but sank anyway,' says Linda, opening her eyes and looking over at Maria, who has turned away and is muttering the word 'Titanic' to herself.

'The Titanic, yes. What happened to that glass of water?'

'I dropped it on the floor.'

'That was clumsy,' says Linda, propping herself up on the bed and catching sight of the glass. 'But it's not broken.'

Maria grabs the glass agitatedly, and heads for the bathroom. Linda can't take Maria's fear any more. Her own fear is enough – or is it perhaps anger that she feels the most? Or powerlessness? She doesn't quite know what she feels, but whatever it is, it's exhausting. Linda pretends to be asleep when Maria comes back. She hears her put the glass on the bedside table, and then feels a hand on her cheek. 'I promise to sing at your wedding, on your eightieth birthday, or when you win a prize because you've saved the world or just because you're amazing. But I'm not singing at your funeral, because you're not going to die yet.'

Linda doesn't answer, though the word 'whatever' floats around in her head.

Maria has stopped stroking her cheek, but Linda can still feel her hand there. She wishes she could open her eyes, smile, and tell her friend that it isn't happening. That she's not going to die. That there's still hope. But she doesn't even believe it herself.

Maria takes her hand away. Linda hears her pick up her jacket and bag from the chair. She half-opens one eye and sees her friend take something out of her bag. It's a medal. Maria ended up with silver in the diving competition. Maria turns and Linda quickly closes her eyes again. She hears Maria put the medal down on the bedside table before heading out of the room. As the door clicks closed, Linda stares after her and says: 'I love you.' Then she turns her head to the window and looks out. It's snowing outside. It always does in February. After all, you don't get spring in February, as her mother always says. Strange that she should think about that now.

Chapter 11

It's their weekly tutor-group period. All the desks are pushed against the walls and the pupils have put their chairs in a semicircle in the centre of the room. The teacher has moved her chair in front of her desk and is sitting with her legs crossed. They've been discussing a class trip they're planning to go on in May. Linda hasn't said a word. She has nothing to contribute to the discussion. The class trip will go without me, she thinks. Linda hadn't known any of the answers in Maths this morning. But that had suddenly been totally fine. And the teacher hadn't made plans for her to catch up with the work she'd missed in hospital. It was as though her Maths teacher had already subtracted her from the future.

'So, are we all agreed then, class? We'll sell cookies, not hotdogs, to raise money for the trip,' says the teacher, uncrossing her legs. She puts her hands on her knees and gets up. 'And you should all calculate the number of boxes of cookies you think you can sell.'

'Minus me,' says Linda.

It just pops out of her mouth, and she looks about her, as though she's as confused as anyone else in the room about where the words came from.

'Well . . . hm,' says the teacher, with an awkward little laugh. 'It's a long time until May, and I've talked to your parents, Linda. And, well, perhaps you'd like to say something to the class? I mean about why you've been away for a week?'

The teacher sits back down. One foot tucked behind the other. Does she need the toilet? thinks Linda. Or is that how adults always sit if they're pretending to be laid-back, when they're really shit-scared? Linda takes out the brown envelope. She's had it tucked under her chair, waiting for the moment when she says – she's not really sure what. Maria suddenly lets out a sob. Linda takes the X-ray out of the envelope, and entwines her feet in the same toilet-needy way as the teacher.

'This is how my heart looks,' begins Linda, gazing out over the class. She feels her mouth go dry and the sweat dripping. For some reason she is only sweating under her left armpit. The body's a weird thing, she thinks, realizing that she's smiling.

'Wow!' says Henrik, the number-one class idiot.

'Twat,' hisses Oscar, then flashes a smile at Linda.

Yes, and that's Oscar, my boyfriend, thinks Linda. Whom I shall love with the whole of my mangled heart. She stuffs the X-ray quickly back into the envelope.

'But that's just a picture. It doesn't really tell you much. It just says that I have to take things a bit easy. But only until I get a new one . . . a new heart, that is,' says Linda.

'Yeah . . . like someone's going to give you a new heart!' scoffs Henrik.

Linda acts like she hasn't heard.

'But actually, I wanted to tell you all something completely different. It's my birthday on Saturday, and I'm going to be thirteen and stuff. So I'm having a party the day before, on Friday. It's at my house. And everybody's invited.'

'Cool!' says Markus.

'But is your home big enough?' asks Maria. 'For the whole class?'

'Sure. We'll have it in my granny's old flat. There'll be a karaoke competition, and a disco, and a DJ and no adults. Will you all come?'

'Yeah, sure!' says Oscar, smiling and looking round at the others in the class. Everybody nods and says that of course they'll come. Everybody apart from Henrik, who is staring at Linda with eyes narrowed like slits.

'Okay, everybody,' says the teacher. 'Put the desks back, please. And remember; lift them, don't drag them! Chop-chop!'

Linda goes over to her bag and puts the X-ray in the inside pocket.

'You're lying,' says Henrik, sidling up to Linda.

'What am I lying about?'

'About getting a new heart. My mum's a doctor and she says it's almost impossible to get a donor; I mean, somebody that can give you a new heart.'

'I know what a donor is. Do you think I'm stupid?' snaps Linda.

'But you're going to die!'

'Henrik! Linda! Can you help clear the classroom, please? Well, perhaps not you, Linda. Henrik, you can put Linda's desk back as well as your own.'

'Because you're going to die soon,' whispers Henrik, with a sneer.

'I can always hope some idiot meets with an accident. You, for example,' Linda says spitefully.

Chapter 12

When the class plays indoor hockey Linda has to sit out up in the stands. She's brought a book with her, but instead of reading she finds herself looking down at Henrik and secretly wishing someone could give him a hearty jab in the ribs with their elbow. If only she could have played too, then she'd have done it herself. She can't help smiling at the thought of him doubled up on the ground.

Oscar is running about down there too, with his freckled legs poking out from under his knee-length shorts. Suddenly he gives Henrik's shin an almighty whack with his stick. Henrik howls with pain. Oscar shouts an apology, before looking up at Linda. He did it for me, thinks Linda. He's really rather sweet, she thinks, smiling and waving down at her new boyfriend.

Suddenly a pair of Dr. Martens boots appear beside her, and wearing them is a boy. Linda eyes travel up to his face. It's the boy. He offers her his hand.

'I'm Zak,' he says.

She takes his hand.

'Linda.'

'You're the best,' says Zak, sitting down beside her.

'How do you mean, the best?'

'At indoor hockey.'

'No better than the boys.'

'Being aggressive isn't the same as being good. You strategize.'

'How do you know that? How long have you been following me?' asks Linda, feeling a sudden pang in her chest. She's nervous of this Zak guy, and yet she feels drawn to him. Which is why she doesn't get up and go, but remains sitting.

Zak ignores her questions. He just looks at her. It's the same look as he had on the tram and at the swimming pool.

'What do you want?' she asks.

'Let's go outside,' says Zak, getting up and buttoning his long black coat. It's the coat that makes him look like some sort of emo kid, along with his pale face and the fact he looks like he's wearing make-up.

'I'm not allowed. I've got to sit and watch.'

'Just leave.'

'The teacher will go ballistic.'

'Nobody will say anything, I promise. Just get up and leave,' says Zak, winking at her.

Linda shuts her book and puts it in her rucksack. When she looks up again, Zak has gone and the door onto the playing field is sliding quietly closed. She stands up with her rucksack in her hand and gazes at the door. Then she swings her rucksack onto her back and very quickly, so she can't change her mind, sneaks over to the exit.

'Look, Miss! Linda's leaving!' shouts Henrik. She'd like to shove his face in dog turd.

'Henrik, let's concentrate on what we're doing. Come on,' says the teacher before blowing the whistle. Linda glances over her shoulder, and sees the teacher dropping the ball to continue play. So the sports teacher has erased her from future consideration too, thinks Linda.

It's freezing cold out. Linda stops on the steps outside the gym, pulls up the zip on her jacket, and puts on her woolly hat. Squinting in the sharp winter sunlight she catches sight of Zak. He's over by the fence with his back to the sun. She walks towards him. As she gets closer, she can see that he's playing with a lighter.

'So, what do you want?' asks Linda.

'To remind you that you're going to die.'

'Thanks, but that's really not necessary.'

Zak succeeds in igniting the lighter and holds one hand over it, lowering it towards the flame and holding it there. Linda feels sure she can hear it hissing.

'Doesn't that hurt?'

Zak doesn't answer. He just looks at her as she watches his hand. It's almost as if she can smell burnt flesh. He closes his hand around the flame and extinguishes it. Then he puts the lighter in his inside coat pocket, before showing her the palm of his hand. It looks totally fine.

'I thought you'd be more grateful,' he says eventually.

'Hmm. Thank you for saving me,' says Linda. 'It was you, wasn't it?'

'Well, yeah. But I was thinking more about the fact you cheated death,' says Zak, looking away.

Linda doesn't answer.

She looks down at her shoes. The toes are scuffed. If she'd polished them more, they might have lasted another year or so. That's if she didn't grow out of them first, of course.

'Yes, death; the great mystery. It's hardly strange that you're afraid,' says Zak.

'Stop it.'

'How long did the doctor give you? Ten months, ten weeks, ten days, ten minutes, ten seconds? Come on, how big was the lie?'

'He said it might be okay. You said it yourself, I cheated death,' Linda protests.

'So he gave you hope?'

'I might get a new heart.'

'But then someone else has to die, have you considered that?'

Once again Linda's eyes wander to the tips of her shoes. Maybe it's not too late to clean them, a bit of black shoe polish and they'll be as good as new. Zak grabs her around the wrist and drags her towards the car park. She tries to tear herself away, but he's a good deal stronger than her.

'What do you want? Who are you, really?'

'I'm your new best friend.'

'I didn't ask for a new friend,' says Linda, digging her heels into the gravel so he's forced to stop.

'Admit it, you are a bit curious,' says Zak, without letting her go.

'I need to get back to class,' says Linda, even though he's right; she is curious, and she does want to go with him. It doesn't really matter where to, she just wants to get away from school.

'Why should you go back in there? Haven't you noticed that they're already treating you as though you're dead? You're not in the script for the future – that's why they don't give you any hassle.'

'I'll get into trouble,' says Linda, feeling her resolve weaken. The grip around her wrist loosens.

'No, you won't, and do you know why?' says Zak, letting her go.

Linda shakes her head.

'Because they're scared of you.'

'How do you mean?'

'They're scared of you because you're going to die. And looking at you reminds them that they'll die too one day. You remind them that life is just a matter of chance.'

'You're not nice,' says Linda, turning away.

'At least I'm honest.'

'So is Henrik.'

'Sure, but he's a turd.'

'And you're not?'

'Do you think I smell bad?' Zak smiles. He reaches his hand out to her. Linda hesitates before taking it. His hand is cold. He pulls her closer. He's right; he doesn't smell the least shitty. In fact, he doesn't smell of anything at all.

Alright, she thinks to herself. I'll go with him. I'll take the chance.

*   *   *

Zak has lent her his helmet and now she's riding on the back of his moped, arms round his waist.

'Can't you feel it?' Zak yells over his shoulder. He's wearing her woolly hat. She doesn't know any other boys who would casually stick a girl's hat on their heads.

'Feel what?' she shouts back, feeling laughter erupting inside her. For the first time since the dive she feels like laughing aloud.

'That life is good! All you have to do is hit the accelerator,' says Zak, putting his foot down. He leans forward over the handlebars and Linda leans with him.

'Isn't this fun?'

Zak laughs. Linda laughs. And their laughter and the hum of the engine fuse as they whizz along the quay.

Suddenly she realizes that he's driving straight towards the fjord.

'Watch out for the edge of the quay! Are you mad?'

'What if you didn't have long left? Wouldn't you wish you could fly for those last few seconds? Ten, nine, eight, seven . . .'

'Stop! I want to get off.'

'. . . four, three . . .'

Linda feels her heart spluttering and stuttering again.

Dunk, de-de-dunk, dunk, de, dunk. She sees the edge coming closer.

'. . . two, one, zero . . .'

They fly into the air, and the moped disappears from beneath them. Linda shuts her eyes. Her heart is juddering like an old engine.

Chapter 13

Linda shoots through the water like an otter. She tries to come to the surface, but there's a hand clutching at her foot. Linda backs away, trying to get loose. Then she sees Axel's face in front of her. His lips are moving. Although she can't hear him, his words reach her: I've missed you.

'Hi!'

It is Zak's voice. Linda opens her eyes and looks up at him. There are snowflakes floating down from the sky, gently hitting her face and melting, but otherwise she's completely dry and still in one piece. They haven't landed in the water after all. Zak has snow in his hair, and he is caressing her cheek.

'Am I dead?'

'What do you think?' he answers.

He plonks himself down so hard that the wooden surface beneath them rocks. They've landed on a floating jetty below the quay. Did Zak know it was here? Had he planned this? Linda feels her body all over. It doesn't hurt anywhere. Zak gets up and stretches out a hand to help her up. She pretends not to have noticed and scrambles up on all fours.

'Where did the moped go?' she asks.

Zak smiles, and tosses his head back towards the water.

'My God, you're crazy. I was sure that was the end,' says Linda, creeping to the edge of the jetty, and looking down into the sea. She breathes in the faint smell of salt and seaweed, but can see nothing other than her own reflection in the still water.

'It was only a moped,' says Zak.

He stands behind her on the jetty, legs wide apart and hands on hips.

'You scare me,' says Linda, sitting back down on the jetty.

'Good.'

'Good?'

'Yes. That means you'll forget to be afraid of all the other stuff.'

'You mean, that I'm going to die.'

'Well, strictly speaking you've already been through that.'

'What do you mean?' asks Linda, tucking her knees up under her chin.

'In the swimming hall, of course.'

'I don't really remember much. But I suppose that might be true,' she says hesitantly, before falling silent and resting her chin on her knees. Even though it's snowing, she isn't shivering. 'But it was as though I saw everything from a bird's-eye view. And I saw you too. I saw you running towards me, and I saw you smash your fist into my chest. It was that punch in my chest that saved my life,' says Linda, looking up at him.

'You just left your body,' Zak says matter-of-factly, as though that was a daily occurrence.

'Was that why you looked up at me? You were the only person who looked up. Everybody else was busy looking down at my body,' says Linda, aware of her growing curiosity about Zak.

'That's right. But how did it feel to leave your body?' he asks enthusiastically.

'It was . . . peaceful. As though everything down there, all the drama, was meaningless and unimportant.'

'Were you frightened?'

'No, not then. Or yes, when I realized I was about to die, I was frightened I might not come down to my body again,' says Linda, looking down at her hands. She looks at her nails that are bitten right down. Maria is always telling her off about it, but she puts her right index finger in her mouth and chews her nail a bit more, before continuing: 'And later, in the ambulance, when we were on the way to the hospital, I was terrified.'

Linda can see the whole scene before her. And she feels the same chill go through her body as she felt when she saw her parents: sitting close together in the ambulance, their faces so thin, their mouths like pale, narrow streaks, her mother's hand clutching at the edge of the blanket that lay over her, the nervous flashing light and the screech of the siren. Yes, that was when she'd been seriously scared.

'I got frightened when I saw Mum and Dad,' she says.

'You caught their fear?'

'Yes. And perhaps it sounds stupid, but it was as though there was a wall between us. And that wall seemed to grow even bigger when I was in the hospital. There I was, on one side of it, while Mum and Dad and the rest of the world were on the other.'

Linda looks down at her shoes. She thinks how there's no need to worry about their scuffed toes any more. She can only repeat what she has already thought; that she is free to polish them or leave them, because strictly speaking there's no point any more.

'That wall only exists in your head. You can decide to make it disappear,' says Zak.

'Yeah, sure. Perhaps you could tell me exactly how I'm meant to do that?' says Linda, feeling herself get cross. She's had enough of this Mr Wise Guy act.

'Aha, are you feeling angry, Linda? Good,' he says, crouching down beside her.

'Hmm. A part of me just wants to lie in bed, pull the duvet over my head, and wait for the day to pass,' Linda sighs.

'And what if everything suddenly passes by while you're lying there? Including life itself?'

'I know . . .'

'Do you want to hear a story about a woman I knew?' asks Zak, continuing without waiting for an answer. 'Well, this woman had been warned by a fortune teller that she would die in a road accident. At first she was terrified, but then she thought of a way to cheat death. She decided never to go out of the house. She stopped visiting her friends, stopped going to the cinema or the shops. Then one day a truck came speeding along, swerved off the road and plunged into this woman's house. So she did die in a road accident, even though she was sitting in her own living room.'

Linda looks down. Zak gives her a little poke in the ribs and laughs.

'So, you see, Linda, there's no way of cheating death, and luckily nobody knows exactly when, where or how it'll happen.'

'That story: I don't think you really knew that woman,' says Linda.

'Does that matter?' asks Zak, getting to his feet again. 'Haven't you got a birthday party to get ready for? It seems there's an awful lot to prepare before Friday.'

'Who are you?'

'I'm the person who's going to take you home,' says Zak, stretching out his hand. This time Linda takes it, and he pulls her to her feet.

'You're so cold,' she says, pulling her hand away.

'It's February,' he teases.

'And it isn't spring yet, in February.'

'That's right,' says Zak, clambering up onto the quay.

Chapter 14

Linda is lying on her bed staring up at the ceiling. She is fully clothed. Covering her is a small knitted patchwork quilt. It's too small, really, since it was made for her by her grandmother when she was a baby. Around her neck is a swimming medal. The one Maria gave her when she was in hospital. Linda looks down at the floor, and at the brown envelope that's lying there. The X-ray of her heart is sticking halfway out of it. Linda thinks how weird it is that she can't actually see what's wrong in the picture. She leans over to pick it up, but a hand reaches it before she does. She looks up and sees her mother standing over her.

Her mum takes the heart picture out of the envelope, and looks at it. She has a deep furrow in her brow. It's not one Linda has ever noticed before. Is it a new wrinkle? Is it because of her? These questions make her feel nauseous, flitting through her mind together with a chilling disquiet. Will her mother wake up one night and start to bleed like last time? Will it be Linda's fault if there's no baby again?

'Have I slept for a long time?' asks Linda, knowing the answer from the darkness outside.

'A while. We're going to eat soon. Dad's made his speciality. Spaghetti carbonara!' says her mother, sticking the picture back in the envelope and putting it on the desk.

'Mum, are you frightened?' asks Linda.

Linda suddenly realizes that it frightens her just to ask the question, so she tries to look calm as she folds up the little quilt and puts it on top of the pillow.

'We've got to be strong,' says her mother, staring straight ahead.

'That wasn't what I asked,' Linda replies, trying to catch her mother's eye.

'Okay, yes. Yes, I am frightened. Frightened and angry. Mostly angry. It would have been easier to bear if it had been me instead.'

'But I don't want you to die,' says Linda.

She wants to add that her mother *can't* die now. Not when she's pregnant. But the fact that her mother might be pregnant is the giant elephant in the room.

'Nobody's going to die, darling. We'll get through this.'

'Everybody's going to die. Nobody escapes death,' says Linda.

'When did you get to be so smart?' asks her mother, trying her best to laugh.

'After I died.'

'Linda, don't say that.'

'But it's true. I died there in the swimming hall. And you mustn't be afraid if it happens again, because it was peaceful. It wasn't painful or anything.'

Linda doesn't know if she even believes it herself, but she

feels responsible for not making her mother too sad.

'It shouldn't be *you* comforting *me*,' says her mother, perching on the edge of her daughter's bed. She reaches out to touch the medal that's hanging around Linda's neck. Linda sits up and lifts the red-white-and-blue ribbon over her head so her mother can take a proper look at it.

'Maria gave it to me. I don't suppose there'll ever be any medals for me; silver or gold.'

'But you have a heart of g—'

Her mother stops herself mid-sentence. She gives back the medal to Linda and gets up.

'Come and have some supper now.'

'A heart of gold? Is that what you were going to say? It doesn't help to have a heart of gold when it's a mangled wreck.'

'Well, you've cheated death once. You are Mummy's little superhero.'

'You know something, Mum. I'm not sure I can cope with all that any more. I've been thinking of making a list of all the things in my room, and deciding who should inherit them. Will you help me?'

'Can't we talk about that later?' says her mother. Linda can see she's frightened and upset.

'Do you think everything stops when we die?' Linda asks more gently.

'Don't think about that now. Come on, dinner's ready.' Her mother stretches out a hand to lead Linda out into the kitchen.

'Five minutes.'

'Are you too tired?'

'I'll come in five minutes.'

'Okay, see you in five,' says her mother.

Linda waits until her mother has shut the door behind her, then swings her feet out onto the floor. She sits with her hands resting on her knees, before pushing herself up. She pauses, standing listening to her body; her heart is still hacking away: no change there.

She goes over to her desk, opens one of the drawers and takes out a piece of paper. She looks at it. It's the list she and Maria made; the list of all the things they should do when they get to be teenagers. It's a good list. Not quite logical, but perhaps she can still achieve some of the items on it? She reads down the list:

Kiss
Travel unaccompanied by adults
Go to parties
Go to a rock concert
Bunk off school
Wear make-up
Do something (a bit) dangerous
Dive from the Black Cliff
Experience real love
Do something exciting

Linda takes a felt-tip from her pencil case and puts a ring around 'Go to parties'. And she's already bunked off school, so she can cross that off. She folds up the piece of paper and puts it back in the drawer before going to eat her dad's spaghetti carbonara. Not that she has any plan of showing her parents this list, but it might just be easier for them if they saw her doing some of these things, instead of dwelling on the idea that she's going to die.

Chapter 15

'Is it too salty?' asks Linda's father looking over at her. She is pushing her spaghetti round her plate.

'Erik,' says her mother, placing a hand on his arm. 'It's delicious. Absolutely delicious, isn't it, Linda?'

'Mmm,' says Linda, twisting some spaghetti round her fork and stuffing it in her mouth. Her father smiles before shovelling some into his own mouth too.

'Was it nice to be back at school today?' asks her father.

'Hmm,' says Linda, with her mouth full.

'I expect everyone was glad to see you.'

Linda swallows her food and rolls her eyes. She reaches for her glass, and takes a massive gulp of water, allowing it to slosh about in her mouth before swallowing.

'Linda, manners!' her mother reminds her.

'I'm having a party on Friday,' says Linda, leaning back in her chair and crossing her arms.

'Oh?' says her mother, flashing a glance over at Dad, who in turn looks back at Linda.

'You haven't forgotten it's my birthday on Saturday,

have you? I'm going to be thirteen!'

'Of course we haven't. But we thought we'd just have family – and Maria too, of course,' says her mother, looking over at her father again.

'Yes. And we could rent a good film and make something special to eat. And have a nice cosy time.'

'I don't want a cosy time, I want a real party,' says Linda. Her parents' suffocating care is even worse now. Especially when they're trying to act so normal. They're so bad at it, they make it ten times weirder than it needs to be.

'Right. How many people were you thinking of inviting?'

'I've already invited my whole class. Plus the other class in my year.'

'But that's nearly forty people. How are we going to fit them all in?' protests her mother.

'We can go down into Granny's old flat. It's empty. If we push the furniture to the sides in the library, we can have a dance floor in there, and I want karaoke and not that horrid home-made pizza, but the kind you order from the takeaway and lots of cakes and sweets . . .'

'Yes, but Linda, is this such a good idea?' says Dad. 'The doctor said you had to take it easy. Avoid stress.'

'A party isn't stressful, it's fun.'

'But forty people! I'm really not sure,' says her mother.

'Oh, please. I'll only be thirteen once in my life!'

'Well, it might be nice for all of us,' says her father, glancing hesitantly towards her mother, '. . . to have a party?'

'Mmm, maybe. And the flat has been empty for a long

time. And it's not important, now, exactly when we redecorate it.'

'Is it going to be redecorated? Why? Don't say we're getting more of those stupid students in.'

'No,' says her father, putting his hand on her mother's shoulder. 'We've other plans for it.'

'Oh? Like what?' says Linda.

Why can't they just hurry up and say it? But no, she's not getting a straight answer out of them.

'We'll talk about it another time, Linda. Right now, we have a party to plan. It's not long till Friday.'

Her mother doesn't even look at Linda as she says it. Instead she and her father sit there gazing at each other, so that Linda suddenly feels as if she isn't in the room at all. It's as though the wall between them has returned. The wall that Zak says only exists in Linda's head. So she decides to break through it.

'I need a thousand kroner,' she says.

'What? A thousand kroner?' says her father.

The invisible wall collapses instantly.

'What do you need so much money for?' asks her mother, taken aback.

'I'll need to buy loads of stuff for the party; balloons, confetti, snacks, a nice dress.'

'But a thousand kroner?' her father protests.

'Nice dresses don't come cheap.'

'Alright! But I'll come with you,' says her mother, getting up from the table. 'Dad can tidy up, and then take his girls out on a shopping trip.'

Linda pushes her chair back from the table too. She picks up her plate, scrapes the leftovers into the bin under the sink, and rinses it.

'I'll go to the shopping mall with Maria.'

'But it would be fun for the three of us . . .'

'Mum, I'm not a kid any more.'

Chapter 16

Linda is standing in the changing rooms. She holds in her tummy to zip up the dress she's trying on. But she gives up, and pulls a face at herself in the mirror. What was she thinking? That she'd look good? For whom? Oscar? The curtain is pulled back and Maria is standing there, holding three more dresses. She looks at Linda and raises her eyebrows, signalling that she doesn't approve of what she sees.

'That is just so completely . . .'

'. . . so completely wrong. I agree.'

Linda takes the new dresses, and hands Maria the ones she's already tried on.

'Don't forget, I want to see you in all those dresses,' Maria says, before closing the curtain.

Linda looks at the three dresses hanging in front of her. One is pink, which makes it a complete non-starter. The skimpy little green number is out too. She goes for the black one with a wide skirt, the kind that whirls around your legs when you spin round. She wriggles out of the dress she has on, and tries it on. Amazingly, it fits. She gives a little twirl. The curtain is pulled aside again.

'Classic!' says Maria, pulling Linda out of the cubicle so she can see herself in the big mirror.

'Ooh, yes!' exclaims the sales assistant as he walks towards Linda. 'You look wonderful, darling. And I've got a petticoat that would look divine under it. Wait a sec.'

Linda smiles at Maria, and gives another twirl.

'You look so grown-up,' says Maria.

The assistant returns with a petticoat and practically shoves Linda back into the changing room with it.

'You have simply got to have that,' says the assistant when Linda emerges again. 'Lots of people have tried that dress on, but nobody's looked as stunning in it as you.'

Linda twists around, trying to read the price tag on the back. Maria comes over and finds it.

'It's a bit expensive, isn't it?' she says. 'And how much is the petticoat?'

'It's only 250 kroner. Which isn't a lot when you consider how much use you'll get out of it,' says the assistant.

'It comes to 750 kroner altogether,' Maria whispers to Linda.

'I'll take it,' says Linda.

She gives a final twirl in front of the mirror before disappearing back into the cubicle to change again.

Minutes later Maria and Linda are walking arm-in-arm through the shopping centre, Linda carrying the big shopping bag.

'Are you going to regret this?'

'A really gorgeous dress can never cost too much! Wasn't that what the guy in the shop said?' says Linda, laughing, even though she's already regretting it slightly.

'Yes, he did. Now, what else do we need to buy?'

'Some decorations and stuff. We can go in here,' Linda says, turning into a gift-and-party shop.

'What kind of theme were you thinking of?'

'Theme?'

'Yes, for the party. Is there a theme . . . like, say, spring, or love, or princesses?'

'Definitely not princesses! Lets take a look,' says Linda, walking between the shelves of paper tablecloths and serviettes. If she's honest, she doesn't know what to choose. She wants it to be nice, but all these serviettes and things just seem so boring. Maria taps her on the shoulder, and she turns.

'How about fancy dress?' Maria asks, peering at her from behind a pair of plastic glasses attached to a big nose and moustache. She offers a clown nose to Linda, who puts it on.

'And with false noses, everything's suddenly alright?' says Linda.

'Hey, you two!' A grumpy-looking teenager shouts at them from behind the counter. 'This is a shop. If you want those things you'll have to pay for them.'

'Yeah, sure,' says Linda.

She grabs a packet of balloons and some streamers disinterestedly, and then heads towards the cash desk. 'Can you choose some serviettes, Maria?'

Linda dumps her purchases on the counter and the grumpy teenager starts tapping them into the till.

'Do you want that nose too?' he asks, pointing his finger rudely into Linda's face.

'Yes, please. But I think I'll keep it on,' she says, backing away.

'That comes to twenty kroner.'

'Not too expensive for a new nose!'

They've still got some money left after their shopping spree. So Linda treats them to some ice cream. They each sit on a plastic stool, eating in silence. Linda still has her clown nose on.

'Are you okay?' asks Maria.

'Apart from the fact that I should have chosen the pistachio instead of the lemon sorbet,' answers Linda, scraping the bottom of her tub.

'Linda, I just wanted to say . . . I was so scared at the swimming competition. I thought you were going to die.'

'So did I,' says Linda. She tries to throw her empty tub into the rubbish bin, but misses, and gets up to put it in.

'But seriously, Linda, I love you to bits.'

Linda turns towards her friend. Maria's barely touched her ice cream. And she's sitting there with tears in her eyes. Linda feels a dark clump growing in her chest. This isn't fun. Doesn't Maria realize that all this crying just makes things worse? Linda has to swallow back her own tears before answering.

'Please don't look so miserable. I survived, didn't I? And there's no point being miserable before I'm gone. You can cry a bit afterwards, but not now,' she says, trying her best to be gentle.

Maria suddenly bursts out sobbing. Linda takes off the clown nose and walks over to her friend. As she puts the nose on Maria, it hits Linda that it's the second time in just two days she's had to comfort someone. She wipes a tear from Maria's cheek with the sleeve of her jacket.

'Are you so ill you might die?' Maria asks.

'I'm so healthy I might live.'

Linda takes a piece of paper out of her pocket.

'Here's the list.'

Maria takes it from her.

'Look, I've already crossed out "Bunk off school". And I've put a circle around "Go to parties".'

'Why do you have to have such a big party? Wouldn't it have been better with just you and me, and Oscar and Markus?'

'As if!' says Linda, rolling her eyes.

'Yes, but . . . but is it good for you? I mean isn't it going to be stressful for you to have such a big party?' Maria asks, with tear-filled eyes.

Linda gets up, grabs her friend's tub of ice cream, chucks it angrily in the bin and puts her hands on her hips.

'I'm trying to put it out of my mind. And that's really hard with you sitting there bawling your eyes out. Can't you see that?'

'I just thought . . . that list . . . is it really that important any more? Isn't it a bit superficial?'

'What's wrong with being a bit superficial? I want a party. I just want everyone to be happy and to have a good time.'

Linda grabs the nose again and puts it back on herself. 'Can't you see I'm trying to cheer you up?'

Maria doesn't answer. She just shifts uneasily, dries her tears and gives a sigh.

'Nobody will mind.'

'But I mind!'

'Please don't be cross.'

'Why not? Are you worried that I'll die if I get too worked up? That my heart will suddenly stop?'

'Linda, don't be horrid.'

'Horrid! I'm not being horrid! I'm in a great mood. I'm wearing a red nose, I'm going to make everybody happy, and we're going to have an amazing party on Friday. Everybody will have fun!'

Linda can feel the dark clump growing and growing in her chest as she talks. If she's not careful, she'll burst into tears herself. So she swallows hard, turns around and marches off.

'Linda! Linda! Where are you going?' Maria shouts.

The tears have started to roll down Linda's cheeks, so she waves quickly over her shoulder and walks straight through the shopping centre, and out through the swing doors, into the dark where nobody can see.

Chapter 17

Down beside the harbour, the carrier bag containing her dress slaps against her knee with every step Linda takes. Stopping outside a cafe she peeps in at all the people sitting there in the light. She catches sight of the semi-transparent reflection of herself in the window. That's how everybody seems to see her nowadays; like a vague shadow that might disappear if they blow a bit too hard or say something wrong. Do they know how they make her feel? Her parents? Maria? Her teachers? Her classmates? That the more they tiptoe around her, the more she feels as though she's fading into the distance. Disappearing.

She almost wishes she'd died in the swimming hall. Then at least she'd have been in the papers, like the girl in America. Linda can see the headlines now: GIRL'S HEART STOPS IN THE MIDDLE OF A DIVE or DRAMATIC DEATH-DIVE. But there won't be any headlines now; she'll probably die quietly in her bed, or in some other insignificant or boring way. Linda sighs as she stands at the window. Nobody in the cafe seems to notice her. It's almost as though she doesn't notice herself. The red nose is the clearest thing about her, and that isn't even real. Linda is about to take it off when she feels a hand on her shoulder.

'Hi.'

She turns. It's Zak.

'Do you make a habit of sneaking up on people?'

'You're the saddest clown I've ever seen.'

'I'm not a clown at all. I just make everyone miserable.'

Linda takes off the nose and hides it in her hand.

'No, you don't,' Zak protests.

'Yes, I do. Everyone feels so sorry for me. That's why they've agreed to come to my party. Because they all think I'm going to die soon. And Mum gave me money for a really expensive dress. Nobody's acting normal.'

'Have you thought they might be coming because they like you?'

'Hmm,' Linda grunts.

'Let me look at that nose.'

Linda opens her hand. Zak immediately sticks the nose on and does a little pirouette.

'Was that impressive, or what?' he says. 'Reckon you need a clown at your party? A clown who can make cute little balloon animals? And who can make people laugh?'

Linda sighs, but can't help giggling. It feels so liberating to be with Zak. He's the only person who doesn't act strangely because of her illness, who helps her forget to be scared.

'Or would that be childish?' he says, grinning and taking off the nose.

'Wow, how *did* you guess?'

'Shall I tell you a secret?' asks Zak, whispering into her ear. 'I'm extremely good at guessing things.'

Then he tickles her and makes her laugh again. It's so good to laugh. It's as if all the woolly, grey gunk inside her loosens and melts away.

'You see. I guessed right . . . you're ticklish.'

'Are you any good with music?' asks Linda, realizing that she's forgotten to invite Zak to her party. The person she maybe wants to be there more than anyone.

'Me? Sure! I'm good with everything!' says Zak, thumping his chest with his fist. 'Why?'

'Then that's your job. I need a DJ on Friday,' she says, suddenly breaking into a wild sprint down the quayside. She doesn't give a damn about all the warnings to take it easy; she just wants to feel alive. And when do we feel more alive than when we're running?

Chapter 18

Linda stands there feeling amazing in her new dress, although it perhaps looks a bit over-the-top with the tiara Maria insisted on her having. Her birthday tiara. Today – or to be precise, tomorrow – she is thirteen. Zak hasn't turned up, or rather he did turn up but he left again, muttering something about some other engagement. He provided her with a playlist and now her dad tries to act as DJ. He has put on a baseball cap and a pair of horrible sunglasses. It's slightly embarrassing, but no one has commented on the fact that her father is the DJ, and the music is precisely as it should be: a bit too loud so nobody has to talk. The big creamy birthday cake would have been enough to keep everybody quiet anyway. Plastic spoons are scraping paper plates for every last crumb. Some people are looking greedily towards the cake-stand, wondering if there's enough for seconds. Henrik is the first to pile more onto his plate, but once he's started, everyone else follows suit. Linda can't even manage her first slice. She mashes up what's left on her plate so it looks like she's eaten more of it. She looks at her father squinting into the computer screen, concentrating on Zak's perfect playlist, trying to be the cool dad.

'Your doing great, old man!' Linda leans towards him and giving him a thumbs-up.

'My pleasure,' he answers, not lifting his eyes from the screen. 'I've got some great tracks lined up, Linda. I hope your guests are ready to let rip.' Dad looks up and grins.

Linda ducks down and pulls a carrier bag out from under the table. Then she gets up onto a chair and signals to dad that he should bring the music down.

'I hope everybody's had enough cake, because now it's time to dance. Lower the lights!'

Oscar leaps over to the dimmer switch and turns the lights low. Linda reaches into the bag and takes out a miniature disco-ball and a torch. She hands the torch to Maria who switches it on and shines it at the little disco-ball, so that flashes of light scatter across the room, but mostly on the birthday girl herself, who is fixing the disco-ball under the ceiling lamp.

'This may not be the world's biggest disco-ball, but it's time for some action!' shouts Linda. But as Linda jumps down from the chair, she stumbles. The bodies in the room freeze. Linda steadies herself and shakes her head, making the tiara go wonky.

'Don't worry! Only joking!' she says, laughing as convincingly as she can.

Daddy sends her an insecure smile before he turns up the music, and Linda shoves the chair to the side and starts swaying her hips. You've got to go for it, she thinks to herself, starting to wave her arms above her head too. Maria puts away the torch and does the same. Oscar and Markus are the first two boys to venture out onto the dance floor. But soon everybody's bobbing up and down and singing 'we will rock you'. It may be a really old track, but it's brilliant to shout to.

As she jumps up and down, Linda can feel the necklace that Oscar gave her for her birthday dancing against her skin. And she can feel his gaze too. She turns to him, touches the little dolphin charm that hangs from the chain, and smiles. He smiles back and comes closer, his cheeks flushed. He's right up close now. As a slow track begins, Oscar takes Linda's hand. Linda looks around for Maria, and sees her nodding encouragingly.

But Linda pulls away from Oscar. She grabs an empty 7-Up bottle and shouts that it's time for spin-the-bottle. Dad turns down the music, to the protests of a few couples. Henrik, who has glued himself onto Ella, does nothing to hide his annoyance.

'Spin-the-bottle! How childish is that?' he says, with his hand firmly planted on Ella's bum.

'Shut up, loser,' says Markus, thumping Henrik in the back of his head.

'Weed,' says Henrik, pushing Markus with his free hand.

'Everybody sit on the floor in a circle!' Maria orders, sitting herself down.

Everybody follows suit, all apart from Henrik.

Linda kneels down in the middle of the circle.

'New rules!' says Linda, looking around her. 'I'm the only one who spins the bottle, and I'm the only one who gets to ask the questions!'

'They're stupid rules,' says Henrik, looking for support. But when nobody shows any sign of agreeing, he sits down like the others.

Linda gazes around the circle. Most people have already got their eyes fixed on the bottle, and those who meet her gaze are quick to look away, either at their neighbours or at the floor. Linda sets the bottle in motion. It spins quickly a few times before slowing down and finally stopping to point at one of the girls in the other class.

'Sofie, if I die now, how will you remember me?'

'Are you sure this is a good idea, Linda?' whispers Maria.

'Shh. I'm the one asking questions round here. Well, Sofie?'

'Your dress, and how amazing you look right now,' says Sofie.

'Tonight doesn't count. It's got to be a memory from before.'

'I'm sorry,' says Sofie, biting her lip. 'Er . . . your pink jacket. The one you had at junior school.'

'You are soo wrong! I have never had a pink jacket. I hate pink,' Linda says, preparing to spin the bottle again.

'Am I out, then?' asks Sofie hesitantly.

'No, you just sit there.'

Linda spins the bottle again.

'Tina?'

'That's easy. You put a worm in our teacher's salad once. It was disgusting,' says Tina, giggling, and making everyone else laugh too. Linda grins with satisfaction. She wants to be remembered for being funny and tough.

She sets the bottle in motion again. This time it stops in front of a small, skinny boy from the other class.

'Kristian?'

'Kristoffer,' he says.

'Oh, yes!'

Linda suddenly thinks that Maria might be right. Perhaps this game isn't the best idea after all.

'My name is Kristoffer, and I remember you pushing me into a pond in year 5. Then you told everybody I'd wet myself. And it wasn't true.'

'But you must have realized it was a joke,' says Linda, reaching for the bottle. I don't want to hear anything more from that wimp, she thinks. The blood pounds in her ears, and she can feel them going red. Typical.

'And last year you put ants in my lunch box.'

'Oh, c'mon! Is that such a big deal?' says Oscar, with a sigh.

'She forced me to eat them. It was disgusting. And for the rest of the day everybody called me an anteater.'

'But it was just a bit of fun,' says Linda faintly. She knows she never apologized, and she remembers threatening to beat him up if he told. Just don't think about it, she says to herself. Just forget it! Just suppress it. But one person who hasn't forgotten or suppressed it is Kristoffer, and right now he's like a dog with a bone.

'But just because you find things funny, doesn't mean other people find them funny!' says Kristoffer. His voice grows louder and cracks on the last word. There's a red rash appearing on his neck.

Linda doesn't answer. She is about to spin the bottle again, but Kristoffer grabs it and holds it tight.

'But she didn't mean any harm. Did you, Linda?' says Maria, leaning forward and loosening Kristoffer's grip.

'Won't you even say sorry?' asks Kristoffer, glaring at Linda.

'I'm sorry,' says Linda, unable to meet his eyes. 'I'm sorry, I'm sorry.'

Then she gets up and as she leaves she can hear Kristoffer shouting after her, asking if she really means it.

'Yes,' she says. 'I really do mean it.'

But she can't bring herself to face him as she says it.

'Thank you,' she hears Kristoffer say.

Linda doesn't answer him. She just runs out and slips into the bathroom. Then she locks the door behind her.

Chapter 19

Through the door Linda can hear that the music's gone back on. She stands with her eyes closed, and sniffs the comforting fragrance of her grandmother's perfume that still seems to hang within the walls of the flat. What would Granny say if she were here now? If she knew what kind of person Linda really is. Just the thought of it makes her eyelids sting. Linda wishes her guests could just disappear, and be gone when she comes out. She wishes she could turn the clock back. She sees Kristoffer before her, and all those faces around them. Faces that say: is this guy out of his mind? Or do they say the opposite? Perhaps these faces say: what an awful thing to do! Linda's so bad; it's good she's going to die! Had Linda really been so unaware that she was upsetting Kristoffer? No, she has to admit it had occurred to her. It's just that it was so easy to do. So tempting. Can she help it if there's something about Kristoffer that screams out to be picked on? He gets so easily worked up. And then it's all the more fun. Anteater! Everybody else had thought it was hilarious. Nobody said it was wrong. Whoops, that's not entirely true;

Maria had been cross with her and hadn't talked to her for days.

Which is why she knows it's Maria who's standing outside the door now. She can sense her presence, even though Maria hasn't said a thing yet, or even knocked on the door.

Perhaps that's why her heart stopped? Because she's too despicable to be allowed to live? Because she's the kind of person who bullies weaker people to make other people laugh, so she feels she's tough and popular.

She takes out her mobile. No new messages. Not a thing from Axel. Her birthday isn't actually till tomorrow, but still. She brings her hand to her neck and touches the little dolphin charm from Oscar. Poor Oscar. Does he know she's only with him to get some practice with boys? That she doesn't really love him? She closes her eyes, her fingers still clutching the dolphin. She imagines Axel; the sun reflecting in the saltwater droplets that scatter onto his face like rain. She can almost feel herself treading the water, his breath against her cheek. His hand tucking a lock of wet hair behind her ear. His lips parting. She can feel herself pull back because she thinks he's going to kiss her.

'You're like a dolphin,' he said, before diving down below the surface and disappearing. And now here she is, wearing a dolphin necklace that's been given to her by Oscar. It's all wrong. She gets up and puts her phone into camera mode, and takes a selfie. From above. It makes your eyes look bigger if you gaze up into the lens. She stares at the picture. She looks so innocent, wearing her tiara and pretty dress. And with the angle of the picture it seems as if she's got a bit of a bust. Everything's just fake. She sits down on the toilet seat and writes a text under the picture.

'Hope you haven't forgotten it's my birthday tomorrow? Dolphin-girl.'

There's a soft knock at the door. Linda looks up from the text.

'Yes?'

'It's me. Maria. Are you alright?'

'Yes. Wait a minute,' says Linda, erasing the message.

She takes a square of toilet paper, moistens it under the tap, and wipes away the smudgy mascara from under her eyes. Then she throws the paper in the toilet and flushes it, before unlocking the door.

'Linda, what are you doing?'

'Who knows? Having a party?'

'Everybody's wondering where you are.'

'Everybody thinks I'm a bitch. Has Kristoffer gone?'

'Yes,' says Maria, stroking Linda's hair.

'Hmm. I'd forgotten what happened. But he's right. I did pick on him. I thought it was fun. I didn't even consider his feelings. They weren't important. It was the same when I hid that worm in the teacher's salad. All I thought about was making other people laugh. I'm an egotistical monster. Why do you even hang around with me? Why does Oscar want to be my boyfriend? And why did everybody come to my party?'

'Because they like you. And I like you. Don't you get it?'

'But I'm not a nice person. And the worst thing is, I didn't have any bad conscience about picking on Kristoffer. Even now, I can't stop thinking he's a bit pathetic. But he's right. I did bully him. And I'm not even sure if I've apologized in the right way. What's the right way to apologize?'

'But Kristoffer accepted your apology,' says Maria.

Linda doesn't answer, but lets her friend put her arms round her. It's easy for her, thinks Linda. Maria is so perfect. She's popular without being cool or tough.

'What's it like to believe in God, Maria?'

She doesn't quite know why she's dragged God into the conversation suddenly. Perhaps because she's behaved so badly. Perhaps that's when we need God most. So we can say sorry and believe that he's sitting up in Heaven somewhere, scratching his chin a bit, before smiling kindly and saying: 'That's alright, my child.'

'It's a good feeling, I suppose. But then I don't have anything to compare it with. I've never had to make an effort to believe in God, if you know what I mean.'

'Ever since I was told I could be cured if I got a new heart, I've been fantasizing about accidents. Imagining that someone with a suitable heart is killed, so I can have their heart and live on. Do people who believe in God think like that too?'

'Linda, I want you to live too. I also want you to get a new heart.'

'Perhaps you could include it in your prayers one night? When you're having a chat with God?'

'I already do. But perhaps you should try and talk to Him yourself?'

'I don't know how. Where do you get to this guy? In church? Or what?'

'He's everywhere. But mostly, he's in your heart,' says Maria, placing a hand on Linda's chest.

'Hmm, that's what you think!' says Linda, gently pushing her friend's hand away. 'Let's go back to the others.'

'Linda . . .'

'Yes?'

'I love you. I really do.'

'I know,' says Linda.

Chapter 20

There's still music and dancing out there in the room that Granny used to call the library. The Pet Shop Boys' song 'Together' is playing. Daddy looks up from the computer screen with a concerned wrinkle between his eyebrows. Linda smiles and gives him a second thumbs-up for the evening. She can see him breathing out in relief before he puts on a slower track. The bodies on the dance floor shift tempo. They seem to hesitate, unsure if they should desert the dance floor or find another body to dance closer to. Henrik does not hesitate, he zooms in on Ella like a heat-seeking missile.

Linda feels a hand on her arm. It's Oscar.

'Do you want to dance with me?' he asks.

'Alright,' she whispers, letting him lead her out onto the dance floor. He puts his hands gently on either side of her waist, and she puts hers on his shoulders. They are face-to-face.

'That's a great dress,' he says.

'Thanks.'

And then she'll ask me, 'Do I look OK?' And I'll say, 'Yes, you look wonderful...' Oscar and Linda both smile; Linda because the words of the song fit so perfectly with what Oscar just said about her dress, and Oscar because – well heaven knows why, and she's not about to ask.

'Shall we dance a bit closer?' he asks.

'Alright,' she says, feeling Oscar's arms closing about her. His hands are on the small of her back, his chest touching hers. There's barely any air between their bodies, but there are exciting smells. He's used a shampoo that smells of summer, but a deodorant, or something, that smells more manly. Perhaps he's borrowed it from an older brother. Does Oscar have an older brother? She doesn't even know if he has brothers or sisters. She can feel his heart beating. Can he feel hers? The tip of his nose is near her neck. Can he smell that she's wearing a bit of her mother's perfume? They sway to the music. Should she close her eyes? She keeps them open.

'Is that nice?' he whispers into her neck.

Linda nods. She feels his hand slide a little lower down her back. She closes her eyes, but behind her eyelids it is Axel she sees. And it's Axel's voice that she hears through the music. The voice that says again: 'I've missed you.' She lets out a sigh.

'Are you okay?' Oscar says.

'Yes, I'm fine.'

He loosens his hold of her a little, so that they're face-to-face again. He gazes at her. Linda wants to close her eyes. She does. And she moistens her lips carefully with the tip of her tongue.

'Yoo-hoo! Kissey-kissey-kissey!' Henrik is suddenly screeching in Linda's ear.

She opens her eyes in time to see Markus pushing Henrik to the floor.

'Stupid prat!' shouts Markus.

The light suddenly goes on, and Linda's mother appears by the door. Henrik stands up, doing a theatrical limp.

'I was just . . . er . . . I was just joking,' Markus mumbles.

'I see,' says Linda's mother looking around. Dad turns off the music, and she turns towards him with angry eyes, clearly blaming him for letting things get out of hand. 'Well, everybody, it's half past ten now, and I hope you've all had a good time. Some of your parents are already here to pick you up.'

Oscar is still standing next to Linda. She can feel his fingers gently touching her arm. It's giving her goosebumps.

'Shall we see each other some day, maybe Sunday?'

'Sure,' she answers, without looking at him. Her mouth feels like it's full of cotton wool.

'Maybe you can come over to my house? You can have a go on my PlayStation.'

'Er . . . sure,' says Linda.

'I hope you liked the necklace.'

Linda nods.

'Bye, Linda.'

'Bye, Oscar.'

Maria stays behind after the others have gone. She clears the paper plates from the table and throws them into a rubbish bag. The paper tablecloth goes the same way. Some of the gold and silver stars that were scattered over the table as deco-ration float to the floor. Linda bends down and presses the tip of her finger onto one of the little stars so it sticks.

'Maria.'

'Yes?' Maria stops in mid-action and Linda reaches out to her and presses the star gently onto her friend's cheek.

'Thanks for being here and helping with the party,' she says.

'Don't be daft,' says Maria, pushing the tablecloth deeper into the rubbish bag to make more space.

Linda stands watching her. Then she takes out the list, which she'd tucked away on the bookshelf.

Maria takes the piece of paper.

'Well, you can cross off "Go to parties" now, at least. How about "Kiss"? I saw how close you and Oscar were dancing.'

'Er, not yet. But we're going to play on his PlayStation on Sunday.'

'Well, it'll probably happen then,' says Maria. 'Markus kissed me for the first time when we were alone in his room.'

'Yeah, sure. But I've been thinking about something else. About what you said in the bathroom. About God.'

'Yes?'

'About talking to God. I was thinking about going some-where to talk to God. Tonight.'

'What do you mean going somewhere to talk to God? I told you God is in your heart,' says Maria.

'Yeah, whatever. He might be in yours. But I reckon I need to go somewhere to find him,' says Linda.

'A church? You know you're always welcome to come to our church.'

'Yes, but I was thinking you might come with me now, tonight.'

'Where to?' asks Maria, looking very sceptical.

'Nidaros Cathedral. Is there a better place to meet God?'

'But surely it's not open in the middle of the night?' Maria protests.

'No, that's why we're going to climb up and get in. I've heard it's possible.'

'You're crazy!' says Maria, shaking her head and continuing to tidy up.

'Please! It's my birthday.'

'No way.'

'Just think how exciting it'll be. Like a secret mission. You, me and the full moon. Look, it says on the list that we have to do something exciting,' says Linda, refusing to give up.

'But it's against the law to sneak into a church in the middle of the night. It doesn't feel right,' says Maria.

'Alright. I'll go on my own!' Linda says, putting her hands on her hips.

'But what if you fall and kill yourself?'

'Would that be such a big deal?'

Maria sighs and shakes her head.

'Please?' says Linda.

'NO.'

'Please?'

'Wow! You girls are very good at tidying up!' says Linda's

mother, beaming and clapping her hands. Linda snatches the list out of Maria's hand and hides it behind her back.

'Hmm, what are you two up to?' says her mother suspiciously.

'Just teenage stuff,' says Linda, pulling down one of the balloons and squeezing it till it pops.

'We can do the rest tomorrow,' says her mother. 'You'd better get home now, Maria. Your dad's waiting for you upstairs in the living room.'

Linda and Maria follow her out into the chilly downstairs hallway. Maria's father is already coming down the stairs.

Linda grabs Maria by the arm and whispers into her ear.

'I'm going to the cathedral tonight, with or without you.'

'Okay. I'll try to sneak out.'

'I'll be there at midnight.'

'You really are crazy!' Maria whispers back.

'I'll start climbing at a quarter past midnight at the latest. Dad's got some old climbing gear in his workshop.'

Linda lies under her duvet fully clothed. It's gone eleven and she's hoping her parents are too tired to sit up and have 'grown-up time'. Fridays don't tend to be a problem; they usually fall asleep in front of the TV at about ten. And tonight they've had to stay up for the party. There's a gentle knock on her door, and Linda pulls the duvet up under her chin.

'Come in,' she says.

Her mother walks over, sits on the edge of her bed and strokes her hair.

'So, were you pleased with your party?'

'It was perfect. Thanks a million. But can we talk about it in the morning? You must be really tired,' says Linda, unwilling to get into conversation.

'It's your birthday tomorrow,' says her mother, continuing to stroke her hair.

'Yes. So it's important I'm on top form,' says Linda, brushing her mother's hand away.

'You know, when you were born and I saw you for the first time it was . . .'

'Love at first sight, I know!' says Linda, rolling her eyes.

'You think I'm being pathetic?'

'No.'

'Are you sure?'

'Well, okay, a bit. It's just you don't need to keep fussing over me. Everything's going to be fine. I feel really fit. Almost as good as before, in fact.'

Her mother leans forward and gives her a kiss.

'I'll never, never let you go, Linda,' she whispers.

'I said everything will be fine. But I need to sleep now. Night-night, Mum.'

'But you've got your jumper on, Linda. Are you cold?'

'A bit.'

'Shall I get you a blanket? I can ask Dad to make you some tea and honey.'

'Mum, stop fussing. Besides, I've already brushed my teeth.'

'But . . .'

'Please, Mum.'

'Okay, okay. Sleep well, then,' says Linda's mother,

stroking her cheek, and then going over to the door. 'Have you remembered to recharge your mobile?'

'There's loads on the battery. Go to bed, Mum.'

'You know we need to stay in contact all the time, in case anything happens.'

'There's only a thin wall between our rooms, Mum. Night-night. I love you both!'

'And we love you too; our big, grown-up daughter. Shall I leave the door ajar?'

'No thanks, Mum. Goodnight for the hundredth time,' she says with a sigh.

Her mother shuts the door. Linda makes herself comfortable with the pillow under her neck. She checks the time on her mobile and lies there listening to the sounds of her parents preparing for bed.

Chapter 21

The west wall of the Nidaros Cathedral, with its statues of saints, bishops and kings, looms high over Linda. The light of the moon playing hide-and-seek among the clouds makes some of the statues look like they're moving. Linda thinks their faces look far too lifelike in this light, and her heart begins beating harder in her chest. But she can't resist staring up at them. Her heart leaps into a gallop when she suddenly sees a figure moving up there among the stone figures. There's no such thing as ghosts, there's no such thing as ghosts, she says to herself. She takes out her mobile. No texts. Why has Axel almost stopped texting her completely? It's five to twelve. She starts to write a text. *Hi Axel! Just five more minutes before I'm a teenager!* She deletes the message until it just says *Hi Axel!* and then tries again: *Guess where I am?* Linda stares down at her message. And even though she's standing there with her mobile in her hand she jumps when it rings.

'Hi,' whispers the voice at the other end. 'It's me.'

'Hi, what happened to you?' asks Linda, knowing that Maria's ringing to say that she's chickening out.

'I'm not coming, Linda. And I think you ought to go home too. Promise me. Please!'

Maria is whispering down the phone urgently, as though she's frightened she might be interrupted.

Linda doesn't answer.

'Linda?'

'Bloody hell, Maria!' says Linda, swearing because she knows her friend hates it. 'You're a such a coward!'

'Linda, stop it. You know I share my bedroom with Anna and she'll notice if I just go off,' whispers Maria.

'But the real reason is that you're a coward and goody-goody. It might have been better if you were the one who was going to die, seeing as you're on such great terms with God and stuff. You could just saunter into heaven!' yells Linda, and as the words tumble out of her mouth, she knows it's an awful thing to say.

'You're being really unfair now, Linda,' says Maria.

Linda can hear the tears in Maria's voice.

'Yes, just cry!' she sneers, ringing off and stuffing the phone in her pocket. It's a wonder Maria doesn't puke at her own goodness.

No sooner has she put it away, than it rings again. She digs it out of her pocket. Surprise, surprise! It's Maria calling back. Linda feels like chucking the stupid thing at the wall, but satisfies herself with dismissing the incoming call.

'Let me guess; you're feeling angry?'

Linda swings round, with the mobile still in her hand. It's Zak. Of course it's Zak. Linda's almost got used to the way he keeps turning up. Nonetheless the hairs go up on the back of her neck.

'Zak! What are you doing here? Are you spying on me or something?' she growls, although deep down she's pleased to have his company.

Zak doesn't answer. He just takes the mobile gently out of her hand, puts it back in her jacket pocket and zips it up.

'There you are. Now you won't lose it on your climbing expedition,' he says, winking at her.

'You've got no business following me. In fact it all seems a bit psycho to me! And how did you know I was going to climb into the cathedral?'

'It's pretty obvious,' says Zak pointing at the climbing gear that's poking out of her rucksack.

He bends down and pulls it out.

'You're not the first person to think about climbing up the walls of the cathedral and in through one of those little doors up there. And, luckily for you, I know which door isn't alarmed. Come on,' says Zak, walking off.

'Wait a moment!'

Linda digs about in her rucksack and takes out a pair of climbing boots. Zak stops, walks back and looks down at them.

'They're too big for you. You'd do better to wear your own shoes. But have you got any carabiners?' he asks.

'I don't know. I just grabbed what I could find.'

'You don't know? I have to say, your climbing expedition seems rather ill-planned,' he says, rummaging about in the rucksack.

'I don't know what a carabiner is.'

'Well, I do. Luckily for you again!' says Zak, taking a heavy metal clip out of the bag. 'We'll need that to fasten the harness to the rope.'

Clearly pleased with himself, Zak slings the rucksack onto his back and heads for the back of the cathedral.

Chapter 22

'Just slip into the harness as though it was a pair of trousers,' Zak instructs her.

Linda does as he says and lets Zak fasten it securely. Having fastened her harness to the thing he called a carabiner, he goes over to the wall.

'But aren't you going to wear a harness?'

Zak just grins at her, and jokingly curls his fingers like tiger claws, before taking the end of the rope in his mouth and climbing the wall like some sort of Spiderman. When he reaches the ledge, he tugs on the rope and Linda walks towards the wall hesitantly. She can't understand how Zak managed to get up there in less than thirty seconds. Where did he place his feet? Where were the holds for his hands? Zak tugs on the rope again.

'Yes, yes, alright,' says Linda.

'You have to keep your weight on your feet; most people make the mistake of taking too much weight on their arms. It's your legs that are the strongest.'

'Okay.' Linda finds a notch in the wall and gets a tiny

foothold. She runs her fingertips across the surface of the wall. She feels some crevasses. If she can make it up the first couple of metres, she'll have more to grab onto further up. She can already feel she's doing it completely wrong; that she's using her arms to pull herself up. But she can't see her feet. How can she trust something she can't see?

'Feel the wall, Linda. You don't need to look the whole way up, just take one step at a time, and the rest will follow.'

'Sure!'

Linda still has her left foot on the ground.

'You've got to believe you can do it,' Zak says, encouraging her.

Linda takes a deep breath, and looks up at Zak, who seemed to climb as easily as if he'd been on flat ground. She puts her left foot where she has a feeling there must be somewhere to grip, and is surprised to find she's right. Then she finds a crack for her right foot. Now she reaches up again with her left hand. She looks up. Zak is kneeling up at the top looking down at her. He nods at her. She feels herself smile. She feels excited; she'll soon reach the easiest bit of the wall. If she can just grab hold of that protruding edge up there to her left, she'll be able to pull herself up. She stretches, stretches as far as she can, and then: her right foot slips, and she starts to fall.

'No!'

Linda's fingertips scrape against the wall and she's glad she doesn't have any long nails to break. She fumbles for something to grab, but she just grazes her fingertips more. I'm going to die now, she thinks.

In a flash she imagines her funeral: a vicar with his robes billowing in the wind, followed by a group of mourners. The wreaths on the white coffin looking as if they might blow away at any moment. At the graveside, the coffin is put onto a kind of platform and then lowered into the ground. Linda sees her parents standing there with their arms round each other. The vicar says a few words that are carried away on the wind, before he scatters earth over the coffin with a little spade.

The vicar takes out a hymnbook and starts singing. His song cuts through the wind and Linda's mother breaks down. Then Linda sees blood running out from under her mum's skirt. It's running down her legs. Oh, no! Not her little brother too!

'No!'

Linda smashes her hand through the lid of the coffin. She grabs something. A hand. A cold hand. She opens her eyes. It is Zak.

Chapter 23

'Take it easy. I've got you,' says Zak, hanging down from the wall above her. 'You were impatient so you forgot to feel the wall.'

'I saw Mum. She lost the baby and I was sure it was a brother,' says Linda, holding onto Zak.

'Well, perhaps it is a brother. Come on now.'

Zak takes a firm grip of her jacket collar with one hand, and with the other he guides her hand to another place she can grip. He holds her tightly until she has both hands and feet in place, and then disappears up again. Linda clings to the wall. Her fingertips are sore and her knee is hurting badly where it smashed into the wall when she lost hold. And, even worse, her heart has gone completely bananas. She could have died.

'Can I climb down?' she whines.

'No way!' comes the answer.

'But I can't do this,' Linda protests.

'Just follow the wall, Linda. You can do it,' he shouts encouragingly.

'I can do this. I can, I can,' she whispers quietly to herself, with her forehead against the cold stone.

'That's the spirit!' Zak shouts, as if he'd heard her.

Linda takes a deep breath, searches for another foothold and something to grab with her hands, and then she's on her way. Up and up. Not as fast or as elegantly as Zak, but she feels certain now that she'll manage it. Nothing can stop her. I am a tiger, she says to herself. A tiger and a spider. A spider-tiger.

'That was exciting, wasn't it?' Zak asks her, when she's finally beside him on the top ledge.

'I thought I was going to die. It was horrible. I saw my funeral and everything,' says Linda, leaning her back against the wall.

'Oh, well.'

'Is that all you've got to say?'

'Yup.'

'I was suddenly sure that the baby's going to be a little boy. Mum and Dad haven't said anything. I think it's because they're frightened they're going to lose it. It's happened twice before. If I die, the shock might make Mum lose this baby too. And then it'll be my fault.'

'No, it won't. If it happens, that's how it was meant to be,' says Zak.

'Well, I can't die before the baby's born, at least,' says Linda determinedly.

'Come on. Let's go inside,' says Zak, getting up.

He doesn't seem the least bit interested in talking about Linda's vision. That upsets her. She'd like him to listen to her at least, and to tell her how wise she is too. Linda's eyes follow him as he balances his way towards a little door. He takes a key from his pocket and unlocks it.

'Where did you get that key?' Linda shouts after him.

'A kind of loan. Now, hurry up!'

Zak opens the door and slips in.

Linda glances down at the ground and feels a knot in her stomach. Oh my God, it's a long way down. How did she manage to climb all the way up here? Closing her eyes, she takes a deep breath and strokes her sore fingertips with her thumbs. Then she opens her eyes again, and edges her way carefully to where Zak is holding the door open. She peers in. It is pitch black inside.

'Wow, it's dark in there,' she says, trying her best to sound cool. But her voice is trembling so much she can't even convince herself.

'It's lucky you've got a torch,' says Zak, fishing out a torch from her rucksack.

'Hmm,' says Linda uncertainly. 'I only wanted to have a little talk with God. Perhaps he can hear me just as well out here?'

'You're not chickening out, are you? I'd never have thought that of you,' Zak teases.

He switches on the torch before signalling for Linda to go in ahead of him. But his eyes glint like reflectors as the light hits his face. She hesitates again. What are you? she thinks. The words flash through her head, but as she opens her mouth to say them, nothing comes out. It's as though icy water had been poured in her veins, and instinctively she moves back, stepping out into thin air. Zak grabs her in an instant, almost before she starts to scream. But even when she's brought safely back onto the ledge, she continues to scream.

Zak takes her in his arms and holds her tight.

'Hush, now. You don't want to wake up the whole town with your screams, do you?'

'Oh, my God! I thought . . .' Linda stutters. She can hear the blood pounding round her ears.

'You're alright,' says Zak comfortingly.

Linda looks up at his face. His eyes look completely normal. She glances down over the side again, but Zak is quick and drags her back from the edge.

'I reckon it'll be safer if we go in,' he says.

He lets go of her abruptly, and disappears in through the door.

'Please, don't go!'

'I'm still here!' says Zak, poking his head back out. 'You take the torch.'

Linda takes it and feels anything but brave as she stoops to get through the little doorway.

'Wait here,' he says, as soon as she's in.

'Please don't leave me,' Linda protests again.

'If I don't leave, I can't come back. I'm only going to fix the lights.'

'But . . . but we've got a torch,' Linda says forlornly.

'Yes, but wouldn't it be better if I went and turned on some lights? Besides, there's an alarm I need to switch off.'

'But what if there are ghosts? Haven't you heard about

the headless monk? Imagine if he comes when I'm here alone.'

'Yeah, just imagine!' says Zak, with an exaggerated shiver, before bursting into laughter and disappearing.

Chapter 24

'Zak?'

Linda's voice is quiet, but the word echoes sharply around the cathedral. Her hair stands on end. She directs the beam of the torch over towards the gallery where Zak disappeared, but can't see any trace of him. Why is he taking so long? She strains her ears, but can't hear any footsteps coming back to her.

'Zak!'

This time she shouts his name, and in an instant she sees something flicker like the eyes of a cat. Oh, my God! she thinks, as she turns off the torch. Her heart is beating uncontrollably now. Her pulse rate must be dangerously high. Perhaps it's so high she'll die? She remembers the doctor who said she mustn't exert herself. But right now she doesn't have a choice. She's got to battle with all these scary thoughts to stop them overwhelming her. Had she seen right? Did Zak's eyes really shine like a cat's? Or perhaps it was just something she'd imagined? What is it about Zak? Is he a ghost himself? That would explain the way he turns up all the time in the weirdest places, and the way she never notices him before he's right next to her. On the other hand, he seems so real. Apart from the fact that he's so cold to the touch. Perhaps he doesn't have blood. Perhaps he's a vampire? They can hypnotize people so as to control them. Perhaps that's why she can never ask him any questions? Or, at least, when she does, he certainly never gives her a straight answer.

Well, she's certainly in a cold sweat under this jacket, and she has goosebumps all over. Aren't these the signals our body sends out when there's danger lurking? She's got to focus now. She pulls the zip of her jacket all the way up to her chin. Not that it helps. She should have brought a warm shawl. But no sooner does she think it than all the scary thoughts close in again. Isn't Zak coming soon? Even if he is something dreadful, she prefers his company to being left utterly alone in the dark. And if it turns out that he really is a vampire, just longing to sink his teeth into her and drink her blood, then so be it.

No! Now she really must focus on something else. Linda takes out her mobile. No new messages. She puts it back in her pocket and sits down. It's cold on the floor, probably dusty too.

Her pocket vibrates. Linda takes out her phone and checks it. It's not Axel. It's Maria: *Are you home yet? Ring me. Can't sleep. Scared something might happen to you. Maria xx*

Linda feels Maria's worry invade her mind. Whiney-Maria. And herself? Bad-Linda? She sighs and starts answering the text: *Sorry. I'm fine. Sleep well babes xxx*

Then the cathedral suddenly fills with light and Linda jumps, dropping the phone on the floor.

'Calm down,' she says to herself. 'Zak will be back soon. Like always.'

Linda decides to send the text later, saving it as a draft. In an effort to calm her nerves while she's waiting for Zak, she flicks through the video clips she has saved on her mobile. She opens one of Axel.

'Wow,' he says into the mobile camera. 'You're wearing a dress.'

'Aren't you going to say how nice it is,' she hears herself say from behind the camera.

'Yes, it's nice.'

'Do you mean it?'

Axel laughs into the camera and is about to say something else, when the video stops and the picture freezes on him, eyes closed and turning away.

Linda feels a hand on her shoulder and flinches. But it's only Zak, of course. He grabs her mobile.

'Who's that? He looks lame! Ha ha ha!' Zak's laughter echoes scarily around the cathedral.

'That's Axel.'

Linda moves for her mobile, but Zak is holding it out of her reach.

'Is that your boyfriend, then?' he asks, teasing her.

'No, Oscar's my boyfriend,' sighs Linda, suddenly aware that Zak has touched on a raw nerve

'But Axel's the one you're looking at film clips of? Very logical,' says Zak, playing the film clip through. When it's over he sits down next to her and gives her the mobile back.

'It's not that simple,' Linda says, turning the mobile over in her hand.

Zak sits quietly, giving her time to go on. She decides she might as well say it as it is: that it's just a mess.

When Linda has finished offloading her heart, she takes the list out of her pocket and gives it to Zak. He gives it a quick glance before handing it back.

'It looks like a pretty good list. But do you really think life is made up of things to be crossed off a list? What are you going to do when everything's been crossed off? Will you be ready to die then? Will you be finished? If so, it might not be a good idea to be so obsessed with completing these tasks.'

'I don't know. I don't know what I should do. I've never died before!'

'That's what you think, at least,' says Zak.

'What do you mean?'

'Maybe you've lived lots of times before. Perhaps the life you're living now is just a dream? Perhaps you're actually asleep and dreaming all this,' Zak says, sounding philosophical.

Linda looks over at him. Does Zak know something? Does he know more than other people about what happens after death? She's aware that she needs something; that, more than ever, she wants some sort of manual, a guidebook to life. Perhaps that's why she can't give up on the list? Because it gives her something to do? Project Death.

Just as she's about to ask him what he actually knows, he winks at her and nudges her.

'Stop being daft. Why can't we just keep to the facts,' she says.

'Like your list?'

'For example, yes,' she sighs.

'So who's going to be the lucky one?'

'What do mean?'

'You haven't crossed "Kiss" off your list yet. Is it going to be Axel or Oscar?'

'I don't quite know. Oscar and I are going to play on his PlayStation tomorrow. So it might happen then. He nearly kissed me this evening on the dance floor.'

'But Axel's the one you think about most?'

'Yes, but Axel lives so far away, and I don't know if I have enough . . . you know . . .'

'Time?'

Linda looks down at her mobile.

'Are you wishing he'd ring or send a text?'

'Well, it's my birthday tomorrow. He might have forgotten. Last year he sent me a present. But this year nothing's arrived in the post.'

'Something might come tomorrow.'

Linda doesn't respond, so he continues.

'Have you told Axel how you feel about him?'

'No, but he must realize, surely?' says Linda, leaning her head against the wall. She thinks back to the summer. She sees herself running down towards the jetty in her yellow dress. The dress she loves so much, but that her mother says is too small and should be thrown away. She sees now that her mother is perhaps right, since as she runs, her red swimsuit shows under the skirt. Down on the jetty she kicks off her flip-flops and pulls off the dress and leaves it in a heap. She waves at Axel who is lying on a blow-up mattress. He's wearing dark glasses, and since he doesn't wave back, his eyes are probably closed. She watches herself dive in. She and Maria have spent hours perfecting this particular dive. A soundless dive that doesn't even leave a ripple on the water's surface. Axel has no idea that he's got company and that a human torpedo is zooming towards the mattress he's lying on. He lets out a roar as the mattress tips over and he lands in the water. The two of them thrash about before their heads finally pop up over the surface. Their faces are so close they can feel each other's breath. Axel brushes away a lock of hair from her face, and tucks it behind her ear.

'Dolphin girl.'

'Turtle boy!' she answers, her body evading him, hands not returning his touch, choosing instead to spurt him with water. She hears her own laughter, and notices that Axel doesn't laugh back. She watches his face fall, sees him turn and swim back to the jetty, pull himself out, shove his feet into his sandals, pick up his towel and t-shirt and walk away. And she sees how, just at that moment, Mia rides past on her bike, and gets off it to walk at his side. Linda stays in the water and swims over to the mattress. She gives it a shove so it floats towards the shore. Axel lost his sunglasses in the water. Perhaps it'll cheer him up if she finds them? Linda takes a deep breath, dives to the bottom, and searches for his glasses.

'No. I probably haven't told him right out,' she says, looking at Zak.

'No, it's not always easy to say the things we should, or to resist saying things we shouldn't.'

Linda nods. She thinks about the mean things she's said to Kristoffer and others.

'Why is it so difficult to be good?' she asks.

'I don't know. But it might be worth trying.'

'What do you mean by that?'

'Well, when it comes down to it, I suppose we're the sum of what we do,' says Zak simply. 'Somebody who does kind things is kind, and somebody who does bad things is bad. Come on. Shouldn't we go on this expedition, now we're here?'

Zak is already on his feet, and he stretches his hand out to help her up. Linda takes it and lets him pull her up.

'Yes, I suppose we should,' she says. More than ever she wants to avoid thinking about the nasty, bad Linda. Nasty, bad Linda who might die.

Chapter 25

'Wait for me!' shouts Linda, as loud as she dares. She doesn't like the way her voice echoes and booms around the cathedral.

'Get a move on, then!'

Zak doesn't slow down, but increases his speed. His open coat flaps after him like a cape. Linda hasn't any choice but to walk faster too, and even though Zak has switched on the lights, she continues to use the torch. There are so many nooks and crannies that the light doesn't reach. She directs its beam over the stone statues. Their gaping faces lean out from the wall and send shivers down her spine. Why did they carve so many terrifying faces? When she aims the torch ahead of her again, Zak has gone once more. She feels a wave of panic and breaks into a run. What if something or someone grabbed her feet now? She'd die of fear.

'Zak?' she says, her voice faint, her heart beating hard. 'Zak? This isn't funny.'

Then something grabs her from behind. Startled, she jumps, then screams. This is the end. She holds her hand to her heart to try to calm it, but she can feel it thumping even through her thick jacket. Is it a ghost? Is it the headless monk who's come to get her because she's entered without permission? Linda feels a cold breath at her neck. She dares not turn round. Even though she's shivering with fear, a river of sweat is running down her back, and she feels she's about to wet herself.

'Relax!' says Zak, gently taking her arm.

'Oh? It's you!' Linda feels the fear replaced with anger. 'What the hell's going on? Weren't you in front of me a second ago?'

'And now I'm behind you. Exciting, isn't it? There are so many places to hide. Tag, you're it!' he says, prodding her and dashing off again.

'Zak, it's really mean of you to keep frightening me. Imagine if my heart stopped again.'

Linda shines the torch towards the gallery. Zak has gone and she can hear laughter. Has he climbed even higher?

'There's no reason to be scared,' Linda says to herself, heading for the gallery. She tries not to look up at the stone faces. They're too lifelike in the torchlight. Surely all these scary faces are a bit unnecessary? Surely it would have been nicer to have a few friendly faces? It is a church after all! Aren't people meant to feel comfortable here? She reaches the end of the gallery. Here, there's one staircase going up and another going down. She feels a little puff of wind, or is it a breath on her cheek?

'Zak, stop it!'

She swings round. But it isn't Zak. Her torch lights up a face that reminds her of her own. It's only a statue, but she quickly flicks the torch off, and stands with it held against her chest, trying to slow her heart.

'It's just your imagination getting the better of you,' she says to herself. But she has no desire to shine the light on that face again.

When her heart rate is almost normal again, Linda decides to take the staircase that appears to lead down to the ground floor of the cathedral. If Zak wants to fly about up there under the roof like some crazy bat, he can do it alone.

She sees a light coming from a side chapel. She is drawn to it like a moth. The soft, warm light comes from a seven-branched candlestick that stands on an altar. Above it is a Christ figure, hanging from the cross with a tranquil expression on his face. Linda walks straight up to the altar and stands on tiptoe so as to touch its feet. But she immediately pulls her hand back; they feel warm. They must have been warmed by the candles, she thinks, trying to reassure herself. Nevertheless, the words 'I'm sorry' slip from her lips. Luckily Jesus doesn't answer.

'Were you frightened of dying?' Linda asks the figure, as she steps back and sits down on the front pew. She can't take her eyes off the quiet and peaceful face. 'Was it simpler for you, knowing you were going to die for all the sins of the world by hanging on the cross?'

Jesus is still silent. And there isn't even a flicker from the candles at the altar.

'I don't suppose dying is such a big deal, when you're sure you're going to be resurrected,' she says, his mild expression triggering an anger in her. 'You're one big con man really; I could have hung up on the cross and looked cool too, if I knew it was going to be like a short sleep.'

'Are you sure?'

The candles on the altar flicker and one of them goes out, as Zak slips onto the pew next to her.

'Where did you come from?'

'I've been here all the time. So you think it was easy for Jesus to die?'

'At least he knew what was going to happen.'

'He wasn't 100 percent sure. But he believed it. Or hoped?'

'Well, that amounts to the same thing,' protests Linda.

'No, because people who believe can also doubt.'

'Well, at least he didn't have to wonder whether he was going to die or not.'

'So you think it would be easier if you knew exactly when you were going to die? If somebody told you that you were going to die exactly five days from now?'

'I don't know. I don't know anything any more. Apart from the fact that I'm frightened. Frightened and tired,' sighs Linda, bowing her head sadly and resting her elbows on her knees.

'Come on!' says Zak, getting to his feet, before she has time to object. 'Come with me.'

'Where are we going?'

'We're going to build up your courage!'

Chapter 26

In front of a door in a dark corner of the cathedral Zak takes out the key again from his inside pocket.

'What's in there?' asks Linda.

'Not in there . . . but down there,' says Zak, putting the key in the lock. 'This is the staircase down to the crypt.'

'The crypt?'

'Yes, where all the dead people are,' says Zak, grinning without a trace of fear.

Linda doesn't feel the same way. Her palms are sweating, a cold shiver goes down her spine, and her throat closes up. She has all the symptoms of someone who's dead scared.

'You mean there are dead people buried under there? And you want me to go down there with you? Thanks, but no thanks!'

'They're not buried at all. They're in coffins that we can open and look into. Isn't that cool?' says Zak enthusiastically, grabbing her hand and dragging her down into the dark. Linda shudders as the door slams behind them. The fact that the light Zak turned on is rather weak and pale doesn't make her feel all that comfortable either.

'Whoops . . . I left the key in the outside lock!'

'You're joking,' she squeals.

'Yup. Come on, let's go,' he says, without letting go of her hand.

Linda admits she's glad to have a hand to hold right now, even if it is rather a cold one.

The staircase is narrow and has a stale, closed-in smell. It feels as though she's breathing in spiderwebs and dust. Linda is sure Zak must be able to feel her pulse thumping in her wrist.

Reaching the crypt, he lets go of her hand.

'I didn't reckon it would be so big down here,' says Linda, hoping her voice sounds normal, as though peering at dead people was something she did every day.

'Well, it is. Come on. Let's see if we can find someone to say hi to.'

Zak goes over to a tomb in a niche in the wall, and pushes the lid to one side. He looks down into it and sticks his hand in.

'You're mad. Please, let's go,' Linda whispers. She can barely breath, every muscle in her body is tense, and the floor seems to sway scarily under her.

'Weren't you the one who wanted some idea of what happens after death? If you come here you'll see what's going to happen to our bodies. If we're lucky, that is.'

'No, thank you!' says Linda.

Backing away from the tomb, she bumps into something and feels it collapse behind her. She freezes. A piece of bone clatters to the floor beside her. She screams. Terror-stricken, she darts over to Zak. The tomb that she's bumped into has fallen apart and she can see the bones peeping out.

'Oh, no . . . what if they're angry?' she whispers.

'Who?'

'These dead people.'

'I doubt it. They've been nothing but bones and dust for hundreds of years.'

He goes over to the coffin and sticks his hand in and fishes out a skull. He holds it up and talks to it.

'What do you say, sir? Are you angry?' he asks.

Zak's out of his mind, Linda thinks to herself. But her mouth is too dry for her to say anything. It's as if her lips were glued together with superglue.

'Did you always talk this quietly when you were alive, sir?'

'No,' answers the skull puppet.

'Zak, I want to go now,' she says, finally managing to tear her lips apart.

'Theses are just bits of old bone. They're not important. There's nothing left here of these people or the lives they lived. You see, Linda, the important thing is what you do before you get here.'

'What do you mean?'

'That it's too late for regret when you're a pile of bones,' Zak says gently.

'But—'

Linda stops mid-sentence and looks into the two black holes that once held eyes. What has she left undone? she asks herself. Although, of course, she already knows the answer: Axel.

'You'd better get your arse in gear before it's too late! What do you say, sir?' Zak asks the skull, which, of course, nods in agreement.

'Stop it! Stop it!'

Zak starts swaying with the skull in his hand, and hums.

'Always look on the bright side of life,' he sings, before breaking into a whistle. Linda has to bite her lip to stop herself laughing. Zak is pleased she's cheering up and continues to sing and whistle, until he suddenly stops and holds the skull to his ear.

'Oh, really? Do you think so?' he asks, looking at the skull that nods back. 'Right . . . I see . . . we've got a message from the other side here,' says Zak.

'And that is?'

'Life, my girl, life is meant to be enjoyed as long as it lasts,' says Zak.

He carefully places the skull on the pile of wooden planks that had, until tonight, been a tomb. Then, as though it's the most natural thing in the world, he picks up the bit of bone that fell to the ground and sticks it in the pile with the others.

'The point is that it's never too late. You exist here and now, so be present in the here and now.'

'That's not true. I am too late,' says Linda, irritated at all the wise-guy stuff Zak constantly spouts.

'But are you really too late?' he says. 'I've seen the way you look at your phone, the way you think about the text that might come, that has got to come from this Axel guy. And if it doesn't? Then what? That list you're carrying around; is that going to help against death?'

Linda sighs. Zak walks over and strokes her cheek. But Linda pulls away, shuddering at the touch of his cold fingers.

'I think it would do you good to have a bit of a laugh. Come on, I've got more things to show you.'

'Like what?' asks Linda, relieved to be leaving the crypt, but uncertain about what else Zak might have up his sleeve. Perhaps he wants to show her something even more horrifying.

'We're going all the way up to the top!'

'Oy!'

'You may well say!' says Zak with a grin, grabbing her hand again.

Chapter 27

Zak almost flies up the long, narrow staircase towards the tower. Linda huffs and puffs so much behind him that she feels quite embarrassed. Her heart feels like it's beating in sticky syrup. Linda tries to control her breath so she sounds less like a decrepit steam engine. Just as she's about to ask for a little break, Zak stops on a landing above her and rests his hands on his knees.

'Pff! I need a break!' he says.

'Me too,' says Linda, panting and wiping her forehead, which is drenched with sweat. 'Uhh!' she says, trying to laugh.

'It's a beautiful building, isn't it?' says Zak. 'Europe's most northerly mediaeval cathedral.'

'It's beautiful, but spooky.'

'Why do you think it's spooky?'

'Well, they say there are ghosts here; that there's a monk who walks around.'

'And you believe that? You saw for yourself that the dead rest quite peacefully in their coffins.'

'I don't know. It's still a bit spooky with so many dead people about.'

'What do you find so spooky about it?'

Linda doesn't reply. She doesn't have a good answer. Why does a pile of bones scare her almost as much as when she nearly fell and killed herself on her way up into the cathedral? Linda looks down at her hands, and gives her fingers a stretch. It's cold, even though they're indoors.

'Can you hear that?'

'Hear what?'

'Hear the complete silence,' he says, taking her hand. He's cold too. They sit down, side by side, and say nothing for a while.

'Do you believe in God, Zak?'

'Which god?'

'Why can't you ever answer a question directly, instead of asking questions in reply?' asks Linda, sighing and leaning back.

'I have to understand what you mean by the word "god" before I can tell you whether I believe in it or not.'

'Okay. Do you believe in a god who lives in heaven and who created the earth and human beings? The usual kind of god.'

'No,' says Zak.

'No?' Is that it? Is Zak finally giving a simple, straightforward answer to something?

'No, I don't believe in any usual god, but . . .'

'Argh! You're off again!' she sighs.

'Well, what about you? You always want simple answers to complicated questions. Can't you just accept the fact that things might be a bit more complex? More fantastical? Am I really meant to give you a yes/no answer to something human beings have wondered about ever since time began?' Zak has stood up now and is waving his arms about, his coat flapping like the wings of a raven.

'Calm down. I only asked what you believed. Surely that's allowed!' Linda protests.

'Yes, I suppose so,' Zak says, sitting back down. 'But one thing I do know is that the people who built Nidaros Cathedral believed in God, or at least in a power that was bigger than themselves. Perhaps that's why we say things are heavenly, when we mean they're beautiful? Because God is in them . . . because God is in everything that's beautiful.'

'Do you think so?'

'It's a nice thought at least, because it means we're in contact with God whenever we're kind or feel happy.'

'You make it all sound so simple. But what about the times when we do stuff that's bad – does that mean we're in contact with the Devil?'

'The Devil, hmm. I think the Devil is just an idea we've come up with, to explain the fact the world isn't always exactly rosy. We need opposites. Just like there's no life without death; there's no good without evil. Agreed?'

'I suppose.'

'Human beings have good and bad in them. It's a compass, in a way, for how we should behave. When we do something right then we feel good, and when we do something wrong we feel bad,' he says, suddenly throwing Linda up onto his back before she has a moment to think.

'Hey! What are you doing now?' she says, flinging her arms round his neck. She can feel that his body is very slender; how can he be so strong? Again, the thought hits her that he might be supernatural, and possibly dangerous too.

'You're very strong,' she says carefully. If he's dangerous it's probably best not to provoke him in any way.

'Thanks. But you're not exactly heavy. Typical girl! Thinking she weighs a ton when she's a skinny little thing!' he jokes, setting off up the stairs again.

When they reach the final landing Zak puts her down. The last flight of steps is too narrow for him to have her on his back.

'Can you manage the last few stairs yourself?' he asks.

'Of course,' she says, following close on his heels.

At the top Zak takes out the same key as he has used the whole time, and opens the door out onto the night.

'Does that key fit everywhere?' asks Linda.

'Seems like it,' he answers.

He stands aside to let her go out first. She has just stepped out when her mobile bleeps in her pocket. Linda feels her heart beat a little harder as she takes it out and reads the text. I want to be the first one to say Happy Birthday Linda! Axel Xxx :o)

'There, you see!'

'What?'

'That you don't need to spend so much time worrying. Well? Are you going to text back and tell him you love him?'

'No. But I've got a plan.'

'Good. But don't worry about your plan just yet. Right now, we're going to look at the moon. And don't forget; the only place we can be is here and now.'

He laughs and gives her a little poke.

'Alright, Mr Wise Guy,' answers Linda.

She glances up at the moon and across the town. She has a plan. A great and wonderful plan that she can't possibly stop thinking about, however much Zak tells her to be in the here and now. She's not going to die in her own bed with a pathetic little whimper. She's going to ride like a knight on a white charger, and fix all those stupid things that happened last summer. If Zak's right about the inner compass that shows the difference between good and bad, hers is now telling her to go south and straighten things with Axel. She can feel the thought soothing her, and when she looks up at the moon again, she can see how beautiful it is.

Chapter 28

Saturday afternoon, Linda stands on the front steps and looks at the doorbell. She has one hand in her pocket. She's fiddling with the clown nose. It's like a soft ball, and it's nice to squeeze. Linda rings the doorbell, then walks back down a couple of steps and puts the clown nose on.

Maria opens the door. She says nothing. Just looks at Linda.

'I'm really sorry, Maria. I'm sorry for being so vile yesterday. You're so kind and always mean well. You are the best friend in the world, and you've unfortunately got the worst friend in the world. Me! I'd do anything to—'

'Oh, stop it,' interrupts Maria, stepping aside to let Linda in.

Linda charges up the steps and kicks off her shoes in the hallway, as she has so many times before. She throws her arms round Maria's neck and gives her a big hug.

'I love you to bits,' Linda says, before releasing her friend and flinging off her jacket. Then she takes off the red nose and presses it in Maria's hand. Maria smiles and puts it on her own nose.

'Come on, Linda, let's go to my room. I'll chuck Anna out.'

Ten minutes later the two friends are sitting on Maria's bed. On the bedside table stand two cups of hot chocolate and a plate of waffles that Maria's mother has made for them, since, as she said, it's Linda's big day today. She even told Maria's annoying little sister, Anna, to stay away and leave the older girls in peace, despite it being her room as much as Maria's. And as if to top it all, Maria's mother has put whipped cream on the hot chocolate. Linda loathes hot chocolate, and can't stand cream. They make her feel sick. But Linda smiled and thanked Maria's mum.

Maria picks up her mug and says, 'Bottoms up!' She takes a big slurp and gets a creamy moustache on her top lip, which she gleefully licks off. Meanwhile, Linda stares down into her mug, watching the cream melt into the hot liquid.

'Ah, I forgot! You don't like hot chocolate! Shall I get you a Coke?' asks Maria, already on her way out.

'No, don't worry. I can have a little sip,' says Linda.

She takes a spoon and stirs the nauseating cream into her hot chocolate, hoping it might improve it a bit. Instead of taking a sip, she puts her mug aside and takes out her mobile.

'I got a text from Axel last night,' she says.

'He seems keen,' says Maria, reading it.

'How would you know?'

'It's obvious! He sits up until after midnight just to be the first to say happy birthday! And then he sends you kisses and a smiley face! Boys don't bother with stuff like that unless they're keen. What did you answer?'

'I didn't.'

'Okay, good. You've got to write something totally neutral. He mustn't start getting ideas. You've got a boyfriend now.'

'But I think I like Axel more.'

'You're sure that isn't just because you can't have him?'

Maria's words hurt, partly because Linda has had so few texts from Axel recently. But there's something else nagging her too. Linda grabs her mug, takes a slurp, and goes into defence mode.

'How do you know I can't have him?'

'Okay, okay. So you can have Axel, but then what will you do about Oscar? You can't just go breaking his heart.'

'And you're saying that now! You're the one who wanted us to get together,' Linda says with a sigh. Maria can be unbelievably thick sometimes.

'But I didn't think it was that serious with Axel,' says Maria, pouting sweetly and taking another gulp of hot chocolate.

'Well, anyway, I've decided to visit Axel this half-term,' says Linda, suddenly feeling defiant.

'But I thought your family were staying in town for the holidays?'

'Who said my parents were coming? I thought you might come down to the south coast with me.'

Linda laughs at Maria, who looks like her eyes are about to pop out of her head.

'And your parents will let you go? Just like that?' says Maria, sounding sceptical.

'Not exactly. But after a lot of nagging, they said I could go with your family to your holiday cottage. Come on, it'll be an adventure. Our first trip all on our own.'

Maria sighs and leans back against the wall.

'It'll never work.'

'Yes, it will. I've planned it carefully. I've told my parents I'm going up into the mountains with you and your family, and now you have to tell your parents you want to stay in town with me. And since I've been at death's door, they're guaranteed to let you stay here with us. Our parents won't know a thing. And if they do realize, we'll already be miles away,' explains Linda, impressed at her own cleverness.

'You are completely mad. Even if your plan works, how do we get there? Flights are really expensive. I don't even have enough money to get the coach out to the airport.'

'I got some birthday money. We can take the bus some of the way, then the train, then the ferry, and then hitch-hike a bit.'

'Hitch-hike?' says Maria, her voice rising to a falsetto.

'Sure, lots of people drive just one to a car,' says Linda, wishing Maria was a bit more daring.

'Do you realize we could be kidnapped or murdered if we hitch-hike?'

'Now you're being negative,' sighs Linda. She's realizing pretty quickly that this is not going to happen. She'll never persuade Maria to do anything so outrageous as to run away.

'I'm sorry, Linda, but I can't go along with this,' says Maria firmly.

'Okay, I'll go without you!' says Linda, with growing defiance. She's damned if she'll let this stop her. And come to think of it, perhaps it would be better to go alone. Then she won't have to put up with Maria's constant whining.

'You're at it again,' says Maria.

'At what?'

'Being mean. Was that why you came here and apologized? Because you wanted to involve me in another crazy plan?'

'Yes, but we wrote on our list . . .'

'I don't care what we wrote on our list! Why can't you just be normal again?'

Linda wants to scream, but takes a swig of chocolate instead. It tastes vile, and the oily globules of melted cream make her retch. Linda doesn't want argue with Maria again. She couldn't bear to fall out with her now. Besides, she needs her friend as an alibi. Maria has got to cover for her so she can get far enough away before her parents realize she's gone.

'I've got to go, Maria. Axel and I are meant for each other. It's just that I never realized it before. And I don't know how long I've got left.'

'Yes, but can't you just call him, or send an email? Do you have to travel the whole country?'

'Puh, it's barely half the country.'

'Well, even so, you can't go. Imagine if something bad happens. Imagine if you meet someone dangerous, or your heart stops again, and you're all alone.'

Maria grabs Linda by the arm, her fingers digging into her, and it hurts.

'Oh, imagine this, and imagine that!' says Linda, wrenching her arm out from Maria's claws. 'Shall I tell you a story? There was this woman who had her fortune told, and it said she'd die in a traffic accident, so she stopped going out of her house. One day a trailer drove off the road and right into the house where she lived, so she died after all.'

'What's that got to do with it?'

'Everything. I don't want sit around taking it easy, frightened that my heart might stop any minute, only for it to stop one day while I'm sitting there shivering with fear. I'm still alive, it would be pathetic to throw it away.'

'You're starting again,' says Maria, banging the back of her head against the wall.

'Starting what?'

'It's like yesterday, when you wanted to go into the cathedral. Did you go, by the way? You didn't answer my texts. I was really worried. I lay awake for ages.'

'Yes, I climbed into Nidaros. Zak came, so I wasn't alone. It was really exciting. I'm finished with being scared, Maria.'

'Are you?'

'Yes, I think I am. But I need you,' says Linda, taking Maria's hands in hers. She kneels down in front of the bed and looks up at her friend. 'I need you to cover for me.'

'But you know I'm bad at lying,' says Maria.

'I'm not asking you to lie. I'm just asking you not to say anything. Please. You're my best friend ever. Better than I'll ever be,' says Linda, kissing Maria's hands. Kissing and kissing them until Maria can't stop herself laughing.

'Alright, alright. But you've got to promise me to stay in contact all the way. Send me texts and call,' says Maria.

'I promise,' says Linda, leaping up and throwing her arms around Maria's neck.

'But what about Oscar?' asks Maria, fixing a pair of stern brown eyes on Linda.

'I'll just send him a text,' says Linda, extracting herself from her friend's embrace.

'Linda, there you go again. You can't dump someone by text!' protests Maria. And again Linda feels her sharp claws in her arm.

'Perhaps you can tell him for me?' Linda suggests, already knowing the answer.

'No! There are limits to what I'll do for you! You'll have to do it yourself.'

'Okay,' says Linda freeing her arm and heading for the door. 'Wish me luck.'

'Good luck, you nutter!' says Maria. Linda can see there's a little smile lurking behind the stern mask.

'You love me anyway?'

'Always,' says Maria.

Chapter 29

'Yay!'

Linda leaps off the sofa in a wild dance of victory. She never knew she was so good at racing games. She has just annihilated Oscar completely. But now she gets a weird sneaking feeling and stops mid-dance. She turns towards Oscar who is on the sofa smiling up at her. He doesn't look the least bothered about having lost so badly.

'Did you let me win?'

'Perhaps,' he says, shrugging his shoulders.

'Why?'

'Because you're my girlfriend,' he says matter-of-factly. He pats the cushion next to him as a signal for her to sit down again. Linda sits in a chair a bit further away, and puts the console down on the table.

'Oscar, I really like you,' she starts. She finds it impossible not to sound like a character in a movie, and right now she wishes she was, and that this wasn't really happening. But she continues: 'And it's not you, it's me.'

'Are you dumping me?'

Linda nods and bites the skin around the nail of her right index finger.

'Aren't we just going out because Maria and Markus are together, and they're our best friends?' she asks gently.

'I reckon we are. Or were,' he says with an awkward shrug.

'So is that alright?' asks Linda, scrutinizing him. He doesn't look in the least upset, and although she's relieved, she wouldn't have minded if he'd looked just a bit miserable.

'Yeah, it was probably a bit stupid,' he says.

'I like you lots, Oscar, it isn't that.'

'And I like you too, but not really in a girlfriend sort of way.'

'That's good,' she says.

She reaches up to unclasp the dolphin necklace he gave her.

'No,' he says. 'That was a birthday present. And we're still friends.'

'Are you sure?'

'Totally. And now I'm going to take my revenge! I'm going to annihilate you completely!' he says, starting a new game.

'That's what you think!' she says, grabbing the console again. She moves back to the sofa to get a better view of the screen. Suddenly she feels a hand on her chest.

'What are you doing?'

'Just touching your boob, so you'll crash your car.'

'You're weird,' she says, shoving his hand away.

'You can talk!'

Oscar shakes his head before focusing on the game again. Linda thinks he looks rather handsome when he frowns in concentration. He's not bad for an ex-boyfriend.

Chapter 30

Linda smiles to herself. Her feet are moving in time to the music in her ears. It's great music to walk to. She smiles even more when she thinks about the way Oscar touched her. Girls are meant to get cross about stuff like that, but it wasn't like that. Oscar is Oscar, and thankfully not her boyfriend any more.

The tram rumbles past and stops on the other side of the street. Then as it pulls away from the stop, Linda sees Zak standing under the streetlamp. In exactly the same place as she first saw him. The sight of him makes her feel even more upbeat. She takes out her earphones and waves and shouts over to him. Zak looks up and waves back, then runs across the road towards her.

'Hi,' he says, bringing a waft of cold air with him in his coat-tails.

'Do you live round here? That's where I saw you the first time.'

'Well, I suppose you could say that. Where have you been? You look happy. Not been kissing, have you?'

'No. I broke up with Oscar, and then he touched my boob.'

'Well, that's the sort of thing boys do,' says Zak, shrugging his shoulders.

'Is it?'

'Of course.'

They start to walk down the road together. They go past Ila Church and cross at the traffic lights, on the red man.

'I've decided to go down to the south coast,' says Linda, after they've made a quick dash for it, to avoid being run over by an angry driver hooting and shaking his fist at them.

Zak shakes his fist back.

'Stupid idiot!' he yells at the disappearing car, before turning towards Linda again to ask: 'Is Maria going with you?'

'No, I'm going on my own.'

'You don't have to. I can come.'

Linda stops and looks at him.

'It's a long way. It's even further south than Stavanger.'

'That suits me fine. There's a girl I know, and . . .' Zak bites his lip and looks the other way.

'In Stavanger? You know a girl in Stavanger?'

'Now you're asking too many questions. Do you want company or not?'

'You never tell me anything about yourself, and I tell you everything!' Linda stops, but he just walks on.

'See you at the station,' he says.

'What makes you so sure I'm taking the train?' Linda shouts after him.

'Well, aren't you?'

He turns to her, continuing to walk, but backwards.

'Have you got a mobile number?' she asks.

'No.'

'Surely everybody's got a mobile.'

'Not me. See you later!'

Zak hurries away. Linda puts her earphones back in and shakes her head. Zak didn't even ask when she was leaving. But then he always seems to turn up at the right time. Perhaps he has telepathic powers. She'll have to ask him, if he turns up on time at the station tomorrow. Not that she expects a straight answer to a question like that.

Chapter 31

s, c, r, a, p. Linda puts her next word on the Scrabble board. Her mother adds an e, making it into SCRAPE. Pleased with herself, she laughs and announces that she'll have the last Jelly Baby, which is already halfway to her mouth.

'But you've eaten nearly all of them,' says Linda, looking at her mother, who gets a slightly guilty look on her face as she bites off its head.

'I'm just so hungry. I haven't been this hungry for ages.' She closes her eyes to savour it fully, and then pops the rest into her mouth.

'When you were pregnant with Linda, Wine Gums were the only thing you could hold down, Ellen,' says Linda's father absently as he looks down at his Scrabble letters.

Linda looks at her father and then back at her mother. Will they say something now? How stupid do they think she is? She's old enough to see what's going on. Or are they afraid? Afraid her mother might lose this baby too? Linda's father adds an e in front of the a and a t and an h on the other side, making EATH.

'That's not a proper word,' protests Linda.

'Yes, it is. It's an old word for easy,' he says, defending himself.

Linda leans forward and looks at her father's letters. She sees he has a D. She grabs it and makes the word DEATH.

'There! That's a proper word!' she says.

Neither of her parents answers. Her mother gets up.

'Perhaps I should refill this,' she says, taking the empty sweet bowl.

'No,' says Linda sternly, grabbing her mother by the wrist. 'Sit down.'

Her mother sits down with the empty bowl in her lap.

'What exactly are you two so afraid of? It's only a word in a game.'

'I just thought we were going to have a nice time, and forget that you're not quite on top form,' says her father.

'It seems like the two of you can't think about anything else. On the one hand you both wrap me in cotton wool, and on the other hand you don't want to talk about it,' says Linda, looking from one to the other. 'Nor this,' she continues, pointing at her mother's stomach.

'What do you mean?' says her father.

'What do you mean?' says Linda, mimicking him. 'I mean that Mum's getting big, and that I'm going to be a big sister. Do you think I'm thick or what?'

'But Linda, darling . . .' says her mum.

'But Linda, darling . . . !' Linda copies her mother angrily. 'Blah, blah, blah. Yes, I might die. I might die today, or tomorrow or in forty years' time. But I don't want you to cheat at games so I win, or to avoid saying things as they are. I just want you both to be normal,' says Linda, sweeping the Scrabble pieces off the board and marching into her room.

In her room she goes straight over to her cupboard and takes out a large rucksack. She keeps her ears pricked as she packs. She hopes that neither of her parents – especially not her mother – will come in to talk to her. She packs as quickly as she can. A few clothes, a couple of photos from her desk, one of her with her parents on holiday in Spain a few years ago, and another of Maria in a pink frame. Then she changes her mind and decides to unpack the photos. It's not only silly, it might arouse her parents' suspicion. She puts the rucksack next to her desk and drops down onto her bed. She feels uneasy. How on earth is she going to sleep tonight? She finds her little quilt, the one her grandmother made, and hugs it, breathing in its old, familiar smell. Should she pack it? No, it'll be too much of a bother. Then, remembering her new dress, she leaps up and opens her wardrobe. She's got to take it, of course. Nothing should be left to chance when she's about to experience the most romantic moment of her life. She looks at her rucksack. Perhaps it's not big enough? She hesitates for a moment, then scrunches up the dress and stuffs it in.

She sits down at her desk and takes out the list. Maria and Zak may not approve of Linda's list, but it gives her a kind of calm to work through it. And calm is perhaps what she needs most on the evening before she runs away. She can cross off 'Do something exciting'. Just the thought of last night's adventure gives her butterflies in her stomach. To think she dared to do it, to actually climb in! She puts a cross by 'Do something exciting', and when she thinks about it, she can cross off 'Do something (a bit) dangerous' too. Imagine if Zak hadn't been holding the rope when she lost her foothold on the way up. Or, even worse, if he hadn't caught her when she was about to step backwards into thin air. She could so easily have died.

Now she's ready for the next thing on her list. 'Travel unaccompanied by adults.' Zak is probably a couple of years older than her, but he doesn't count as an adult. How old is he, in fact? She must ask him. But then he's so good at evading her questions. His age, surely he won't mind telling her that? There's a gentle knock on her bedroom door, and Linda quickly shoves the list under the mouse mat on her desk. She swings round on her chair and tries to look relaxed, leaning back with an elbow on her desk.

'Come in,' she says in a cheerful voice.

It's her mother, of course, who puts her head round the door.

'Shall I help you pack?'

'No, thanks. I've already done it,' says Linda, patting her rucksack.

'Have you taken enough warm clothes?'

'Yes . . . woollies and more woollies.'

'Right. So you're all set up for your trip to the mountains,' says her father, appearing at the door. 'Do you want to take some board games or cards?' he asks.

'They've got all that stuff up at the cottage, and I've taken some books,' says Linda, giving her rucksack another tap. 'Thanks for letting me go.'

'Your boots are by the woodburner, warming up,' says her mother.

'Thanks, Mum. That's really sweet of you.'

It's irritating to have such overprotective parents sometimes, but she appreciates things like having nice warm boots.

'Have you got your recharger?' asks her father.

'It's in my bag. Anyway, I'll only be away a few days, and I've been to Maria's cottage hundreds of times.'

'True enough,' says her dad.

'Yes, but—' her mother tries to chime in, but her dad interrupts.

'Let's leave Linda in peace now.'

'Thanks, Dad.'

She feels awful. Her parents trust her, and here she is about to do a bunk. Perhaps it's a bad idea after all? A bit unrealistic at best. She can't even be sure that Axel's going to be that pleased to see her. Linda gets up from her desk and tries to shake off her negative thoughts. It's going to be a long day tomorrow.

Chapter 32

Linda stands in the hallway dressed and ready to go. On her feet she has the warm winter boots. They feel lovely. What isn't quite as lovely is the way her mother insists on sticking around.

'I'll come with you to the crossroads, then I can have a little chat with Maria's parents,' says her mother, about to shove her feet into a pair of boots too.

'Mum . . .'

'Ellen, dear, it's only a short trip,' says her father, joining them in the narrow hallway.

'Thanks, Mum,' says Linda. 'But I can manage to get to the crossroads on my own. Bye, you two!'

Her mother looks despairingly at Linda and then at her husband, and shakes her head.

'Am I being a bit hysterical? Alright, perhaps I am! But I presume I'll get a kiss, at least?'

Linda kisses her mother and then her father. She feels a bit queasy at the thought of having lied to them. They do, in fact, have good reason to be concerned about her.

'Bye!' she says again. And then: 'Love you both!'

She doesn't wait to hear whether they answer or not. She glances at her watch and hurries on. She'll never get to the station on time; she'll have to run like crazy.

Zak is waiting for her when she arrives breathless on platform 2. He waves before running towards her. The controller is ready to wave his flag. Grabbing Linda's arm, Zak helps her to run faster and together they leap on the train at the last moment. As the door closes behind them, Linda falls. She manages to rescue herself with her hands, but the hard, gritty floor grazes them, her rucksack bangs into the back of her head, and her heart feels ready to explode. She thinks of the doctor telling her to take things easy. If they keep up this pace, she'll die long before they get there.

'Whoops-a-daisy,' says Zak, helping her to her feet.

Linda brushes her hands clean. They sting even though there's no blood. She looks at Zak and attempts a smile. At least they're on their way. He smiles back, before leading her through the carriage.

Linda's head rests against the train window; her eyes are closed as she listens to the music in her ears. Together the music and the swaying train seem to rock her thoughts gently back to the summer. She's with Axel in his room. She has Axel's bass guitar in her lap and he's showing her where to put her fingers. She's concentrating hard, determined to get it right this time. Then she feels his fingertips on her forehead, it's like a confused spider walking about. So she shakes her head and looks up.

'You get a little furrow in brow when you concentrate,' Axel says. 'There, between your eyebrows.'

He shows her with his finger.

'Do I?' she says, touching the place he's pointing at.

'Yes, but it's gone now. I'll put a song on, so you can try to play along with the bass line,' he says, going over to the stereo. He fiddles about and finds a track.

It's the song she's listening to right now. 'Deep Pain' by the Pet Monsters. The train goes into a tunnel. Linda can tell it's got darker, even though her eyes are closed. She opens them and looks straight at Zak. He is sitting in semi-darkness opposite her. He looks wide awake. And although he's not reading a book, or looking out of the window, or listening to music, he doesn't look at all bored.

'What are you doing?' she asks, taking off her headphones to hear his answer.

'Being still,' he says, with a little smile at the corners of his mouth.

'Isn't that boring?'

'No,' he answers.

Linda puts her earphones back in. She turns towards the window, where she meets her own reflection before they come out of the tunnel again. There's no doubt they're on their way now. What will Axel say when she turns up on his doorstep? She has the urge to call him, to send a text and tell him. But that would ruin the surprise. What will he do? Hold her? Lean her back and kiss her? A long, romantic, movie-style kiss? And then she can die there in his arms. Or perhaps it would be better if they cycled to the beach, and as the waves crash on the shore and the wind whistles through last year's grass, he can tell her how much he's missed her, and then he can kiss her. The end. Linda smiles to herself. She savours these future moments as she gazes out of the window.

A motorway runs parallel with the train line. There's a minibus driving along it. Linda bangs her head on the window, trying to read what's written on the big logo that's stuck on its side.

'Pet Monsters,' she bursts out. 'It's the Pet Monsters! That's amazing. I'm sitting here listening to one of their tracks!'

'Really?' asks Zak.

'Yes, they're so cool. Axel's really into them too. I learned one of their songs last the summer. We played it really loud on the stereo, and I played bass along with it.'

'Are they famous?'

'They're amazing! And they have this pyro-show at their concerts, and all this fire spouts out over the stage.'

'Have you ever been to one of their concerts?'

'No, but I've seen one on TV. Imagine if they're playing round here. Just think if we could go to a concert. You'd really love them. I think they're your kind of thing.'

'What makes you think that?'

'Well, they all wear black, for starters.'

'And everyone that wears black has the same taste in music?'

'Yeah, whatever,' says Linda, starting to rummage desperately about in her bag.

'What are you looking for?'

'My list. I've got to have my list. It says "Go to a rock concert". And now maybe we can.'

Zak moves over to sit beside her and grabs her wrist.

'Linda, stop it.'

'Stop what?'

'Stop going on about that list. What do you think life is? Some sort of form, with boxes to be filled out?'

'But I like my list!'

'Why? What is it you like about putting crosses next to things on some random sheet of paper?'

Zak's hand is cold, and his questions make her want to cry. She swallows hard and tries to find a good answer.

'Because then . . .' she says, hesitating. 'Then I kind of know what I'm going to do.'

'How about not worrying so much what you're going to do? How about just being here? That's the really difficult thing to do. If you're always thinking about what you're going to do next, you can't ever really be here now.'

'But . . .'

'Shh. Just be quiet now, Linda. I'll come and see the band with you. They're playing at the town hall at the next stop tonight. We can jump off the train.'

'But how did you know that?'

'I told you . . . I'm very good at guessing!'

'Are you clairvoyant?'

'It was in the papers.'

Zak hands her a newspaper that was on the seat next to him. Linda opens it and reads PET MONSTERS TOURING NORWAY.

'Wow . . . amazing. I'm so excited. It's going to be so amazingly cool!'

'You're doing it again.'

'What?'

'Living in the future.'

'We have to be allowed to be happy and look forward to things.'

'Yes, but it's equally important to let all the things around you make you happy.'

'Zak . . . we're sitting on a train,' groans Linda.

'Yes, but it's a very nice train. Look at what nice seats we've got, right next to the window, and feel how soft they are, and how the train rocks so gently on the rails, and how it's just the right temperature in here. Look at the great landscape that's gliding past.'

Zak has taken both her hands and is crouching down in front of her.

'Feel your breath, Linda. Feel how it's going in and out so calmly,' he says, turning off the music that's seeping out of the headphones.

Linda lets him put her iPod in her bag. She suddenly feels calm, and her hands feel heavy and warm in her lap. It's not that bad just to be here. Zak sits down in the seat opposite her again, resting his hands in his lap. Who is he? She wants to ask him a hundred questions again, but something makes her just sit quietly like him. In total silence, feeling her breath and the amazing warmth of her hands.

Chapter 33

There's a bit less snow here in Otta than in Trondheim, but it's still winter here too. Linda quickly finishes her banana and puts her mittens on again. Zak has politely turned down her offer of a banana, insisting that he's already eaten.

'But that was hours ago,' Linda protests, throwing away the skin. 'Do you want some water at least?'

'Stop fussing, will you! Who do you think you are? My mother?' Zak marches off, clearly irritated.

'Wait for me,' says Linda, gulping down the rest of the water.

Zak plonks himself down on a bench and glowers at her.

'How about we play a game?' she says, screwing the lid back on the bottle.

She sits down next to him, and before he can protest she puts the bottle on the ground and spins it.

'Truth or dare?'

'What do you mean?'

'If the bottle points towards you, you either have to give a truthful reply to a question or you have to do something I dare you to do.'

'That's a stupid game,' he says, stopping the bottle with his shoe.

'Ha! You made it stop while it was pointing at you. Now you have to choose . . . truth or dare.'

'Okay . . . truth,' sighs Zak.

'Is it true that you're going to meet a girl in Stavanger?'

'Yes.'

'Is she your girlfriend?'

'You only get one question. Come on, let's check this town out. There's still time before the concert,' says Zak, getting up.

Linda feels a little bit cheated as she picks the bottle up from the ground.

Zak and Linda walk rather aimlessly across the road. Otta doesn't have much to offer apart from a shopping centre. They're crossing a bridge when something comes flapping through the air. Linda jumps back to prevent whatever it is from hitting her in the face.

'Oh no!' she says, when she sees a little bird lying at their feet. It was just an ordinary blue tit.

Linda touches it with her shoe. When it doesn't move she crouches down to take a closer look at it. It doesn't look as if it's breathing. Its beak is half open. Linda takes her mitten off and pokes it with her index finger. It doesn't react.

'It looks dead,' she says.

Zak bends down to look at the bird too.

'It is dead,' he declares, before straightening up again.

'It's weird that it should drop dead out of the sky like that.'

'Do you think so? It's no weirder than when a person drops dead in the street,' he says with a shrug.

'Well, I've never seen anything like this happen before. Have you?'

'Just because we haven't seen something with our own eyes doesn't mean it doesn't happen,' says Zak, wanting to walk on.

'Don't you get bored with being such a know-it-all the whole time? You sound like you're eighty years old!' Linda snarls irritably.

She squats down and looks at the bird; at the wings that are half stretched from the body as though they were in mid-flight when it died. Did its heart stop? Did it have a mysterious heart disorder like her?

'We've got to bury it,' she says.

'Why? It's only a bird.'

'We can't just leave it lying here,' she says, throwing her arms out.

Zak comes over and picks up the bird.

'Let's throw it in the bin.'

'Now you're being horrid,' says Linda, stretching her hand out to the bird. Zak places the little creature in her palm, soft and limp. She lifts it to her cheek.

'It's still warm,' she says, looking over at Zak, who just rolls his eyes.

Linda looks around at the frozen landscape.

'Where shall we bury it? The ground's completely frozen.'

159

'Do you think it cares? Do you think one of the last things it thought before it fell to earth was "I hope some nice people come along and bury me"?'

'Maybe not, but I still want to bury it.'

'Because this is actually all about you, isn't it?'

'What do you mean by that? That it's all about me?'

'You identify with that bird. It reminds you of when your heart stopped in the middle of your dive!' Zak shouts.

'Now you're being mean. Besides, I didn't die.'

Zak flashes her a glance and starts to carry on across the bridge. Then he suddenly turns around and comes back.

'Okay. Let's bury the poor little thing. We'll bury it so you feel better. That's the reason people are so obsessed with rituals, isn't it? They want to feel better. And when the body's buried nobody has to see it break down and return to the natural cycle. Every single little bit of the dead body.'

'It's so sad,' says Linda, peering down at the bird. 'So sad that it'll rot away.'

'Do you think so? If no birds died, then no new birds could be born. Did you know, the minute that bird came into the world, it started to die? And perhaps it hasn't even realized it's dead. Perhaps it's still flying around. Perhaps only its body is lying here in your hand,' says Zak.

'Do you think birds and animals have souls just like people?'

'Why shouldn't they?'

Linda doesn't answer. She crosses over the bridge and starts to sweep away the snow at the roadside with her foot. She takes a stick and tries to dig a hole in the frozen ground. The stick snaps. She looks around for something else.

'I've got a better idea,' say Zak.

'What? Just throw it in the dustbin?'

Linda is furious. She starts to dig with her hands. Her mittens are getting dirty, but she still doesn't succeed in making a hole. Not big enough to bury a bird in, at least.

'It's a bird, and birds like sitting in trees. We can put it up in a tree,' says Zak.

Linda straightens up and looks at Zak. Has this guy lost his mind now, or what?

'Well, what you're doing now is useless, that's for sure,' he says, pointing at the pathetic little hole in the snow and the broken stick.

'Maybe the bird would prefer a resting place in a tree? Come on, let's try that tree there.'

Zak has already started wading through the snow towards the tree. He stands under it and looks up through its leafless branches.

'Shh,' he whispers. 'Can you hear? There's a little bird singing up there.'

Linda listens carefully. She can hear the song, but she can't see the bird. Then the singing stops, and as the bird takes flight, Linda catches a brief glimpse of it.

'Do you want to put it up there yourself?' Zak asks. 'I can lift you up to the lower branch.'

'Okay.'

Linda walks over to the trunk of the tree.

Zak asks if she's ready. She nods. He grabs her round the

hips and lifts her up. He lifts her as easily as if she weighed nothing. Zak must be pretty strong despite being so skinny. Linda rests the limp bird on a branch close to the trunk. Then she lifts herself up onto the branch and sits next to its little body.

'Goodnight,' she says. She can't think of anything more to say, so she starts to sing. 'One winter's morn the wind shall blast, and you my dear shall breathe your last.'

'Then in the snow I'll shroud your sweet form, till the spring sun my cold cheek doth warm.'

His voice rings out loud and clear, and in the middle of the song he stretches out his arms for Linda.

'You know it . . .' she says, surprised. 'It's hardly the most common hymn.'

'Well, it's one of the nicest funeral hymns I know,' he answers.

'Granny had it at her funeral, so I should have it at mine,' she says.

'Do you think about your funeral a lot?'

'Yes, I wonder who'll be there, and whether my soul will still be around as I'm being buried.'

'Would you like that?'

'I don't know. But it would be nice to see who comes. To see that everyone who loved me was there, and that they missed me. Will you be there?'

'Me?'

'Yes, you. I'd like you to be there.'

'Well, the most important thing now is that I get you to Axel, isn't it?' asks Zak. 'Aren't you coming down from that tree now? Jump! I'll catch you,' he says, with his arms still stretched out.

'But will you come to my funeral?'

'Jump now, and I'll catch you!' he says.

Linda jumps and Zak catches her. Then he lets her down to the ground very slowly. They are standing close together. Zak's lips are almost touching Linda's forehead. He mumbles something quietly to her. But she doesn't quite catch it. She thinks she hears him say something like: 'I couldn't possibly not be there.'

'What did you just say?'

'Oh, nothing,' he says. Then he gives her a quick kiss, before pushing her away almost roughly and heading off.

Linda is left standing alone by the tree. The cold is creeping up over her legs. Her boots are no longer warm, all the woodburner heat long gone. Who the hell is Zak, Linda wonders again. She hasn't seen him eat or sleep or drink. He never seems to go to the toilet either. But even if all these things point to him being a zombie, vampire, werewolf, alien or something worse, he's still the person she most wants to spend time with. In fact she's glad that he came on this trip with her, and not Maria.

Chapter 34

'Oh, no,' Linda sighs, taking out her mobile, seeing she has a text from her mum.

'Did I tell you that I think my mother's expecting a baby?' Linda says to Zak.

'Yes, you mentioned something of the sort.'

'I'm frightened she'll lose the baby if she gets a shock or gets upset. She can't find out I'm not with Maria.'

Linda thinks again about the last time it happened. She and Axel had borrowed the boat without asking, and they'd driven it onto some rocks. She's never even dared mention it to Maria. It's as though she's frightened that if she tells anyone, it'll be her fault even more.

'I wouldn't worry yourself about that, if I were you.'

'That's easy for you to say,' says Linda, then, 'Oh God, Maria's the world's worst liar.'

Linda covers her face with her hands.

'I'm the world's most selfish person!'

'Stop it. I'm sure the baby will be fine. Third time lucky, isn't that what they say?'

'I wish I was a bird. Then I could just fall out of the sky dead too, without thinking so much about it,' says Linda with a sigh.

'But think of all the amazing things people can do, that birds can't. Isn't the knowledge that we'll die some day a small price to pay?' asks Zak.

'Yes, but how about tulip bulbs? They get lots of lives. They go into hibernation in the winter and then get another chance the next year, and the next.'

'Wow! Imagine what fun it must be to be a bulb!' says Zak.

'Oh, shut up, idiot. Perhaps it's the same with people. Perhaps our souls just go into hibernation and are born into new bodies. Perhaps the soul is a kind of spring bulb?' says Linda, suddenly getting philosophical, and feeling rather pleased with herself.

Linda looks over at Zak. She observes again how he's standing there without a hat, without gloves, and with his coat undone. Not that his coat looks exactly warm anyway. Perhaps he's an angel? Is that why he's following her about?

'Is that it? Do we perhaps have an immortal part of us, a soul that continues to exist after we die?' she asks hesitantly.

'The important thing is what you believe. No living person knows what comes after death. That's just how it is.'

'But why?' she asks irritably. 'Wouldn't it be better if we did know?'

'Then there'd be total and utter chaos,' Zak protests, getting heated again. 'Just imagine if everyone was absolutely certain they were going to be born again, they'd probably just go off and kill themselves the moment things got a bit challenging.

Game over, and then a new life in a new body! Perfect!' Zak says angrily.

'There's no need to get cross. I was just playing with ideas. Isn't it natural that I should wonder what happens after death?'

'I suppose so,' Zak sighs, calming down again. 'But one thing we know for sure is that nothing of the body disappears after we die. Everything goes back into the natural cycle. And that goes for every living thing. Do you follow me?'

Linda nods. Zak moves closer to Linda, and suddenly he has the same intense look on his face as he had in the swimming hall. The one he had just before her heart stopped.

'In that case,' he continues, 'it would be odd if what we call our soul just disappeared into thin air, don't you think?'

'So, do you know the answer?'

'Why should I know what happens after death any more than you do?' says Zak, biting his lip. 'Can't I play with ideas too?' he adds.

'Yes, but . . .' Linda hesitates before trying again. 'But you're so strange. And you just did it again.'

'Did what?'

'Whenever I ask you something, you always ask me a question back. You never give me a straight answer. What are you really going to do in Stavanger, for example?'

'I've told you, it's a girl. I want to get to know her a bit better, before . . . Ah . . . forget about it.'

'Why? No! What girl?'

'A very cool girl. The best there is.'

'Is she your girlfriend?'

166

'No. If you really must know, she's my sister,' Zak says, turning and marching off down the street.

'Is that really true?' Linda says, running after him and grabbing his arm. He wrenches his arm away, so she loses her balance and falls backwards. Zak holds her, and again she is struck by how strong that skinny body is.

'Do I look like I'm lying?' he hisses through his teeth.

'No, no, I'm sorry,' Linda whimpers, mostly from the pain of his vicelike grip.

'Okay. So we won't talk about it any more.'

Zak releases her. Linda rubs her arm, but she's not about to give up.

'What exactly are you?'

Zak doesn't answer. He just walks on. She runs up alongside him.

'Are you a vampire?'

'Ha-ha! Very funny!'

'Are you an angel, then?'

'Don't be daft!'

'Are you Death, perhaps?'

This last question makes Zak stop in his tracks and burst into laughter.

'What's so funny?'

'You really think I'm Death? As if death is some sort of weird guy who roams about rounding people up,' says Zak, bursting into hysterics again. 'Of all the superstitions in the world, the idea that Death is some sort of person, has to be the stupidest. The man with the scythe! Ha-ha-ha! Death is just a state of being, just as life is a state of being.'

'Sometimes I don't understand a thing you say,' says Linda, sighing, and this time she's the one who leaves Zak.

She can hear he still hasn't stopped laughing. He's standing there giggling to himself. When she glances back, she sees him shaking his head and wiping the corners of his eyes. Oh my God! It wasn't that funny. Zak must realize he's strange. She's certainly never met anyone like him, at least. She wonders about this sister of his in Stavanger, and what she's like. He wanted to get to know her, is it perhaps a half-sister or something? It'll be exciting to find out, that's for certain.

Linda kicks a lump of ice lying on the pavement. It lands next to a leaflet lying at the side of the road. Connie Larsen. Hairdresser and clairvoyant. What the hell's a clairvoyant? she thinks. She stands beside the leaflet and waits for Zak. Perhaps he knows.

'Have you finished laughing?' she asks sarcastically, as he comes up alongside her.

'Almost,' he says, putting a friendly arm around her shoulders. 'But what have we here?' he says, looking down at the leaflet.

'What's a clairvoyant?'

'Somebody who's very good at guessing the future.'

'A bit like you, then.'

'Not quite. This person professes to be able to actually see into the future.'

'To see into the future? Can't we go and see her then?' asks Linda.

Perhaps this Connie Larsen person could tell her something about Axel? Perhaps she'll tell her that Axel is totally head-over-heels in love with her, and that he'll be over the moon when she turns up, because she's come all that way just for his sake.

'Do you really think it's a good idea?' asks Zak, interrupting her thoughts.

'It's ages until the concert, so we've got to do something. And besides, what's the worst thing that can happen?'

'Well, she might just tell you something about the future that you'd rather not hear.'

'I've met a doctor who pointed at a picture of my heart and said that there's something wrong with it that's so rare they don't even know what it is, and who told me that he wasn't even sure if a new heart would cure it, so nothing frightens me now. Not even a hairdresser who says she can see into the future.'

'You've got a point,' says Zak, stuffing his hands into his coat pockets.

'And besides, I'd like a haircut.'

'I think you're perfect as you are, with long hair,' says Zak.

'Who do you think you are? My mother?' asks Linda.

Chapter 35

The hairdressing salon is in the cellar of a private house. It's not exactly full of clients, and when Zak and Linda come through the door, they find a woman with hair like white candyfloss sitting on a deep sofa browsing a magazine. On the table in front of her, on top of a pile of newspapers and magazines, sits a blue Persian cat, purring. Another lies on the sofa next to her, this one pink. Neither of the two cats seems too pleased at having visitors. They leap down to the floor and hiss at Zak and Linda.

'Hey,' says Linda.

'So, the two of you have come at last,' says the woman with the candyfloss hair, getting up and putting her magazine on the table.

'Unusual cats,' says Linda, unable to take her eyes off the two bundles of fur. The cats open their mouths to hiss again, this time almost soundlessly. They have their eyes glued on Zak, and they are arching their backs. Linda looks over at Zak, who has pulled his t-shirt collar up over his mouth and nose.

'Come on, Cherry and Blossom, there's no reason to get worked up,' says the woman, picking up the cats.

'Thank goodness,' says Zak.

The woman doesn't answer, but gives Zak a piercing stare.

'I'm allergic,' he says.

'You're a strange one, alright. But one thing you're not, and that's allergic to cats,' says the hairdresser.

Linda shudders a little. So she's not the only one who thinks there's something strange about Zak. Perhaps this hairdresser really has got some kind of second sight? Perhaps Linda can ask her what it is about Zak? Since he's always avoiding the subject. The candyfloss woman disappears through the door with a cat under each arm. Linda and Zak sit down on the sofa, and Linda leans towards the table to see if any of the magazines are of interest.

'Zak, what did she mean by that?'

'By what?' says Zak, grabbing a magazine filled with pictures of hairstyles.

'When she said you're strange.'

'If anyone's strange it's her. She's totally weird,' says Zak, flicking mechanically through the magazine. 'Do you have any particular haircut in mind? What about that one?' he asks, showing her a picture of a woman with the world's most boring, mouse-coloured, pudding-basin style.

'Certainly not that one. I want blue hair.'

'Blue?'

'Yes, if it looks good on a cat, it should look pretty good on me too!' says Linda.

'I think dyeing a cat's fur verges on animal abuse,' says Zak, flinging the magazine down.

'So you don't think my cats like being pink and blue?' says the hairdresser.

'Whoops,' says Linda, who hadn't noticed the hairdresser coming back in.

'Well, no. I wouldn't say they look altogether pleased,' says Zak, who doesn't seem the least worried about being rude.

'Why not dye half your hair pink while you're at it?' asks Zak, turning to Linda.

'No, pink would be completely wrong,' says the hairdresser. 'But blue would go with your eyes.'

She offers Linda one of the hairdressing chairs.

'Are you Connie?' asks Linda.

'Yes, that's me. And you are?'

'Linda.'

Linda tries to stretch out a hand, but the hairdressing cape gets in the way.

'Right. And the two of you are travelling?'

'How do you know that?'

'I've lived here for years, and one thing's certain, you're not from these parts,' says Connie, loosening Linda's ponytail and beginning to comb her hair.

'Can you see into the future?'

'I can see what might happen. But then again, everybody has free will. So even if I see, for example, that you've got some kind of big love in store, then you'll be free to ruin the chance or even to turn your back on that special person who's waiting for you.'

'Do you see a big love like that for me?'

'I can see that there's lots of love and romance in store for you.'

'It doesn't feel that way,' says Linda, watching Connie stirring the dye in a plastic bowl. It's a vibrant blue. Her mother is going to get a real shock.

'You just need to open your eyes, my girl,' says Connie, spreading the dye on Linda's hair. She has put gloves on and is massaging the blue right into her scalp. 'Now you'll have to sit with it in your hair for a bit, and then I'll rinse it, and cut it, and blow-dry it and style it.'

'It's got to look really cool. We're going to a rock concert later.'

'That'll be a great experience.'

'Do you know who's playing, then?'

'It's always an experience to go to concert. Would you like a cup of tea?'

'A coffee, please. If you've got some,' says Linda.

'Aren't you a bit young for coffee?' says Connie, looking at her doubtfully in the mirror.

'Maybe . . . but when you have as little time as I do, you have to hurry up and try as many things as possible.'

'You're very young, you've got all the time you need.'

'Are you sure?'

'Everybody has the time they need,' says Connie, going out.

'Weirdo,' says Zak, when she's left the room.

'Shh. What if she hears you?'

'I don't give a damn if she does,' says Zak.

'Perhaps she can tell your fortune too?'

'I don't want my fortune told. And I can't be bothered to hang around here any longer either. I'm going for a walk. I'll meet you afterwards, when you're finished,' he says, getting up from the sofa.

One of the cats has crept back into the salon. It hisses. Zak looks down and hisses back at it. Linda swings round on her chair, just in time to see the cat, with its stomach almost flat on the floor, streaking past her and out through the door it came in.

Connie blow-dries Linda's hair and then she puts some wax on her hands and makes it stand up in spikes.

'That's awesome,' says Linda, sighing with relief. She has to admit she was a bit nervous when Connie started cutting it. She's always had long hair, and has never dared to cut it in case she regretted it.

'There, you're ready for your concert now,' says Connie, holding up a mirror so Linda can admire her new hair-do from every angle.

'Brilliant!' says Linda, nodding.

Connie takes off the cape, and Linda bounds out into the centre of the room. The new haircut has made her feel some-how lighter, as though her hair had weighed a hundred kilos. She goes out into the hall and gets her purse from her jacket hanging on the coat stand.

'No, I don't want anything for it,' says Connie.

Linda looks at Connie and bites her lip. What's going on? Nobody gives things away for free, do they?

'Are you sure?' asks Linda.

'Yes, it was jolly good fun. It's not often someone comes in wanting blue hair.'

'Well, thank you,' says Linda hesitantly. She takes her jacket and goes back out into the hall. Zak's right, this hairdresser does seem a bit bonkers.

'Everything will be just fine. Just believe in love. And don't forget: it can be right under your nose!' Connie shouts after her, as she waves goodbye.

It's very cold out, but Linda doesn't put her woolly hat back on. She doesn't want to spoil her hair. And now she thinks about it, that was all she got out of her visit – a haircut. Connie hadn't said anything that made her any the wiser. In that sense she was a bit like Zak. Strange that they should take such an instant dislike to each other. Or perhaps they disliked each other because they were so alike?

Chapter 36

The cold weather has finally triumphed over vanity, and Linda is wearing her woolly hat pulled down over her ears. And in her ears she has music. She's warming up for the concert with the Pet Monsters' biggest hit: 'Deep Pain'. I never really cared for pleasure, so I smile when your words cut me like a razor. Zak was nowhere to be seen when she left the hairdresser's, and it was too cold to wait, so she started to walk. He knows where the concert is, so they'll probably meet there, Linda thinks, humming along with the track. All Pet Monsters' tracks have piles of energy. It puts a spring in her step.

She always thinks of Axel when she listens to the Pet Monsters. Linda remembers seeing him bending over something he's writing at the desk in his room. His tanned neck against the bright-yellow football shirt that announces he's a Brazil fan. She creeps up behind him and puts her hands over his eyes.

'Linda?' he asks.

'No, it's Father Christmas,' she answers. Then she feels him taking away her hands before swinging round on his chair.

She asks what he's doing.

'Nothing,' he answers, and closes his notebook behind him, before opening a drawer and hiding it away.

'Nothing? Are you writing a diary? That's nothing to be embarrassed about,' says Linda.

'It's not a diary,' says Axel, getting up.

'Well, if it's not a diary then I should be allowed to look. Have you written something about me, perhaps?' Linda leans forward to open the drawer.

Axel grabs her wrist.

'It's just some song lyrics I'm trying to work out.'

Linda twists out of his grasp.

'Let me see, then!' she says, trying to open the drawer.

This time Axel grabs both her wrists and holds her tight.

'No. Go away!' he says.

'Alright,' she says.

He lets her go.

She sees Axel's old guitar lying on the bed, and picks it up. She strums the strings and clears her throat. She tells him she's been writing songs too, and that she's not frightened of sharing them.

'Listen to this: "When I count up to three, I think Axel, Axel, Axel. He's brought me to my knee. And he's called Axel, Axel, Axel!"' she squawks, using the only two guitar chords she knows.

Axel smiles, tilting his head sideways as he looks at her. When he smiles she can see how his canines stick out a bit, making him look like a cartoon character. If he was an animal he'd be a fox. She thinks she can see a hint of red in his face. Is he blushing?

'Yes, very nice,' he says, taking the guitar back and hanging it up on the wall where it belongs. Everything in Axel's room has a place of its own. His room looks like the perfect boy's room in a furniture catalogue.

'I'm off to the kiosk. I expect Mia will want to come too,' he says, heading for the door.

Linda is brought back to the present when her pocket vibrates. She takes off a mitten with her teeth and it dangles from her mouth as she fishes out her mobile and reads the text. She's not surprised to see it's from her mother: Good to hear you got to the cottage safely. *Call you tonight. Love Mum and Dad xx.* Linda doesn't quite know what to write without telling too many lies, so she doesn't answer. She scrolls back to the last text she got from Axel, on the night before her birthday. He hasn't written to her since, and there wasn't a parcel in the post either. He often used to text her several times a day. Not that she's answered his birthday message, but that was only to make him start wondering and imagining things.

'What are you doing, Axel? Are you thinking about me at all?' she asks the telephone before starting to write a text: *Hi Axel, are you ready for a surprise?* She giggles to herself, then deletes the message and puts the phone back in her pocket.

Chapter 37

There's a crowd outside the concert hall. Loud and happy mouths talking and laughing at once, breath hanging like clouds in the frosty air. Linda takes her hat off and with one hand tries to fix her hair. She hasn't got a mirror, so she doesn't actually know whether it looks better or worse, but it feels kind of spiky.

She gets a knot in her stomach when her phone goes off again. Her first thought is that it might be Axel, but it's Maria: *Are you OK, babes? xxx*

Great! I'm going to a Pet Monsters concert!!! xxx

Maria reacts with lightening speed. *What? Pet Monsters?! Awesome! Text me photos of the concert.*

Linda laughs as she reads the message. Maria's almost as big a fan as Axel and her.

Will do. Enjoy playing Ludo at the cottage! ;-) love you, babes xx

'Hello, punk girl,' says Zak.

He's got frost in his hair now, but the cold still doesn't seem to bother him.

'Hi,' says Linda. 'Where were you, Zak? I waited outside the hairdressers, but you didn't show up.'

'No. Shall we go in or what?' he answers, nodding towards the queue that's begun to form at the entrance.

'Sure, but why didn't you come?'

'I lost track of time,' he says with a shrug. 'But I'm here now.'

Luckily the queue is moving quite quickly. Linda tries to puff herself up as much as possible. You have to be sixteen to get in. She glances up at Zak, who looks totally calm, as though he's always sneaking into concerts. Or perhaps he is sixteen. She's about to ask him, when one of the doormen addresses her.

'ID?'

He grabs her by the sleeve of her jacket to make sure she can't slip past him. Actually it's tempting to make a break for it, he's not the scariest-looking doorman in history. He's quite short, with a tiny moustache, and the only thing making him look even vaguely muscular is his down jacket. Which is probably what gives her the courage to brazenly tell him that she's forgotten her ID at home in Trondheim, and that he surely can't stop them at the door when they've come so far?

'You have to be sixteen to get in. And that's that!' says the doorman.

'But I am sixteen,' says Linda.

'Hmm, and the Queen is my mother,' snorts the doorman.

'Is she really?'

'As much as you're sixteen, so just beat it, you snotty-nosed kid.'

'Hey . . . there was no need for that last comment,' says Zak, grabbing the doorman's collar.

'Let go!' the doorman growls from under his moustache.

'I'm sorry, but Linda has travelled all the way from Trondheim. She's a big fan, and besides, she's with me. So I'll take responsibility for her in there.'

'Yeah, cos you're sixteen, eh?'

'As it happens, I am!' says Zak, without letting the doorman go.

The doorman shakes himself free. And now he clearly wants to prove he has some muscle too, because he shoves Zak so he lands on his bum on the hard snow. Linda runs to help Zak to his feet. He rubs his leg and looks far from pleased.

'Oy, you! That was unnecessary!' shouts Zak, brushing off the snow. 'That was totally unnecessary!'

'Go home and watch kids' telly,' the doorman shouts back.

'We're not going to give up, are we?' asks Linda.

'Never!' says Zak, scowling at the queue.

Linda and Zak wait until the doorman is concentrating on the queue again before darting round the corner to the back. They sneak along the wall where the band's tour bus is parked. There's a group of young men standing around the door smoking. Linda recognizes them instantly. It's the Pet Monsters! Oh my God! What should she do? She feels like she's frozen to the spot. But she knows it's now or never.

'Hi!' she shouts, waving at them.

The whole band turn to look at her. One of them looks as though he's about to tell her to shove off, and his body language as he walks towards her is very unfriendly too. It's the vocalist.

'Please, can I have an autograph?' Linda asks. 'I'm a big fan and I've come all the way down from Trondheim.'

Linda smiles as broadly as she can, hoping that she might manage to look cute for once. Right now she wishes she had Maria with her; there's not a soul who can resist her velvet brown eyes and silky voice. The vocalist, who she knows is called Chris, smiles uncertainly and glances back at the others, who nod faintly.

'I suppose so,' he says. 'Have you got anything to write on?'

Linda unzips her jacket, takes her arm out, and rolls up the sleeve of her jumper.

'Here,' she says. 'It's as white as paper, at least.'

'Okay. Have you got something to write with too?'

The vocalist takes her arm. Chris, from the Pet Monsters, is touching Linda's arm! She's got goosebumps all over. She clears her throat to answer him. But her mouth is so dry she can't get a word out. So she just shakes her head, and looks over at Zak, who shakes his head too.

'God, it's freezing out here!' says the drummer. 'Why don't you two come back stage, and we'll see if we can find a pen or something in there?'

'Great!' says Linda, able to talk again.

'So, you sit here when you're waiting to go on stage, do you?' says Linda, instantly wishing she hadn't. It's the kind of stupid thing her mother would say.

'Yes, we sit here and drink, er, lemonade or whatever, and eat peanuts and chat,' says the drummer, Tommy, who seems like the friendliest band member. He always wears dark glasses and looks moody in all the pictures and when he's on stage. But he seems completely different now. Linda decides that he'll be her favourite from now on. After hunting around a bit he eventually finds a permanent marker.

'Wouldn't you prefer to have our autographs on some paper?' he asks.

'No, just go ahead!' says Linda, folding back her other sleeve too, and holding out both arms. When they've finished they turn to Zak, who shakes his head and says he'll give it a miss this time.

'Take a picture of us,' says Linda, taking out her mobile and passing it to Zak.

He looks at her phone.

'You've got five missed calls,' he says, handing it back.

'Oh, it's just Mum. I'll ring her later. Come on. Take a picture now, please!' Linda begs, putting the mobile in camera mode and handing it back to Zak.

'Okay. Smile!' says Zak. 'Or look tough.'

'Take two,' says Linda.

Zak snaps again, and then looks at the picture. Linda goes over to see it too. It's amazing.

'Well, it was great to meet you guys,' says Chris. 'But we'd better get ready for the concert now.'

Linda is determined not to go yet. She has got to find a way of staying a bit longer. Perhaps they can see the concert from backstage or something?

'I've run away!' she says. It just pops out. 'Only for a little while,' she adds.

'Right,' says Tommy, with an uncertain expression on his face.

The others in the band turn away, and Linda realizes she's got to come up with something else. Something better.

'And I'm a really huge fan of the Pet Monsters,' she says.

'Linda, I think they've realized that,' says Zak.

He takes her gently by the arm, but Linda doesn't want to give up. She scans the room desperately, and when she sees the bass lying on a chair, she gets an idea. Not the best idea ever, perhaps. But sometimes you have to make do with a slightly bad idea.

Chapter 38

'I know all your lyrics by heart,' says Linda, pulling down the arms of her pullover.

'Right,' says Chris hesitantly.

'Yes, and in the summer my boyfriend taught me to play the bass line of "Deep Pain".'

She catches a glimpse of Zak, who raises his eyebrows as soon as she says the words my boyfriend. She realizes, of course, that Axel isn't exactly her boyfriend. Or, rather, she knows that he is. It's just that she hasn't told him yet. But she will soon. And then it'll be perfect and very romantic.

'Perhaps we should go?' suggests Zak.

'I can show you,' says Linda, determined not to give up yet.

Chris smiles, and Tommy goes and picks up the bass. He glances at the bass player, who nods and gestures to Linda. The bass is heavy, and the strap is too long for her, so she pushes her hips forward and bows right over it to get a proper grip. She stands with her legs apart and hopes she looks just a bit cool. Then she plays the bass line, and hums the melody.

'Wow, that was good. You've got a great sense of rhythm,' Tommy exclaims, when Linda is finished.

He looks at her and Linda looks back at him. And she sees that he has the bluest eyes in the world, even bluer than Axel's.

'Not too bad,' says Chris, nodding excitedly. 'Can you do any of our other songs?'

'No,' says Linda, shaking her head.

She's about to slip the strap back over her head, but the guitarist stops her.

'Play it again, and I'll sing. Tommy, can you give us a bit of percussion?'

Tommy pulls his drumsticks out of his back pocket and sits on his haunches in front of the table. Then he counts them in. Linda counts like mad and manages to come in on time.

'Cool,' says Chris, when the song is finished. 'Do you play in a band or something?'

'No, I'm more of a sports girl,' says Linda. 'Or was . . .' she adds, quietly to herself.

'Wow, that's even more impressive,' says Tommy.

'Don't suppose you'd like to have a go in the band, eh? What would you say to being our guest artist for that song?' asks the vocalist.

'Are you just kidding me?' she asks.

But every cell inside her is jumping up and down with excitement, every little atom in her is buzzing.

'I could do with a break,' laughs the bassist, Andreas.

'That's a deal then,' declares Chris.

'But there's one problem,' says Linda. 'The doorman refused to let us in, and if he sees me on stage, he'll go crazy.'

'We'll handle that. You two can be our guests tonight,' says the drummer.

Linda wonders if she's too young to be in love with someone over twenty. But Tommy is so fit, and he's written his name on her arm. She's never going to wash it off. Nor the names of the others; she likes them all. Perhaps she's getting as boy-mad as Maria?

Chapter 39

Tommy, the world's coolest drummer, with rings in his ears, tattoos and wild bushy hair, leads Linda and Zak along the corridor and out into the auditorium. It's already crammed with people who have got themselves a good place in front of the stage. Tommy gets hold of the doorman, who still has his big down jacket on despite the heat inside.

'These two are our guests tonight. She's going to play with us for one of the songs, so it would be great if you could help her get a place at the front, near the stage, when the concert starts.'

The doorman's eyes narrow the instant he recognizes Linda and Zak. But he doesn't argue. He just nods.

'Right,' says Tommy. 'Do you two fancy a drink? A Coke? A Fanta? A beer?'

'Soft drinks only!' says the doorman sternly.

Linda and Zak nod in unison. Tommy says he's got to join the others backstage.

'But I'll see you on stage,' he says to Linda, winking at her so she tingles from the roots of her hair to her toes.

Zak tugs her sleeve sharply, to stop her gawping at Tommy's disappearing back.

'Come on, Linda,' he says.

The doorman escorts them to the temporary bar and leans over the counter.

'These kiddies are with the band. They're guests. But they're only allowed soft drinks. Understood?'

'Sure. Shall I put them on the Pet Monsters' tab?'

'Yes,' says the doorman, before turning back to Zak and Linda. 'I'm going now. But I'll come back when the concert's about to start. And God help you if I see you near any alcohol. Understood?'

'Yes, of course,' Linda and Zak say in unison.

'Don't worry about Roy. He's just concerned that everything should run smoothly,' says the barman, before asking what they want.

Zak says he'll be fine with just a glass of water, while Linda takes advantage of the offer of a free Fanta and peanuts. She digs into her bag of nuts greedily and chucks a fistful into her mouth.

'I was starving,' she says, swallowing. 'You want some nuts?'

'No, thanks,' says Zak, not making any move to drink his water.

'But you must be ravenous!'

'I'm allergic to nuts. My throat will swell up so I can't breathe, if I get the tiniest bit of peanut in my mouth,' says Zak.

He puts his glass on the bar. Linda feels sure he intends to forget it there. What is it with this guy? Why doesn't he eat or drink? She remembers the hairdresser's reaction when he said he was allergic to cats.

'You're strange, but are you really allergic?' Linda says, challenging him.

'Lots of things are strange,' says Zak dismissively.

'Well, one thing's for certain – you're very different from me,' says Linda.

'That's what you think,' he says. 'Look, the band's coming on stage. Shall we go and get a good place?'

'Wasn't Roy going to help us find one at the front?' asks Linda, looking round the venue.

'As if we need that grumpy old git!' sneers Zak.

Linda doesn't know how, but suddenly they're right at the front. The Pet Monsters have entered the stage, and everybody is screaming and shouting. Some girls yell out 'Chris! Chris! Chris!' They don't know that Tommy's actually the loveliest band member of all. But he's sitting behind his drum kit with his sunglasses on, so nobody can see his eyes.

'Oh, I wish I could be a rock star,' Linda shouts to Zak, over the roaring noise.

'Why?'

'Just look at how many people admire the Pet Monsters. And how much they love them,' says Linda. 'And rock stars live on in their music, even after they die.'

'Do you think that makes dying easier?'

'It would be nice to know you'd done something people would remember. That had left a mark.'

'But, Linda, do you really think people will forget you when you die?' Zak says, struggling to be heard over the noise of the crowd. 'What about your parents and friends? Do you think they'd miss you more if you sat behind a drum kit with sunglasses on?'

Linda doesn't answer. She feels embarrassed that Zak's realized she's a little bit smitten with Tommy. And Zak seems to notice her embarrassment too, since he takes her hand and gives it a little squeeze. Then he whispers in her ear that she'll get to be a rock star tonight, at least.

'Can you film me on my mobile when I'm up there playing?'

'Sure!' shouts Zak.

But they can't say more, because now the drummer is counting the band in and the concert starts with a crash, literally. Fountains of fire light up the sides of the stage. The band gives it their all. Linda can't stop taking the occasional extra look at Tommy, but not so much that Zak would notice, she hopes. She sings along with the chorus, and the verses too. After the first song, the vocalist introduces all the band, before announcing that they have a guest artist tonight. Linda suddenly feels very hot and then freezing cold, when she realizes it's already her turn.

'Please give a warm welcome to lovely Linda from Trondheim!' shouts Chris.

The audience stamps and shouts, even though they can't possibly know who she is. Zak pushes her up onto the stage. Andreas hangs his bass on her. Chris asks if she's ready. Linda nods, and glances quickly back at the smiling Tommy. He counts them in. Then she looks out over the auditorium. The lights are so strong the audience just looks like a sea. Linda closes her eyes, strikes the bass strings, and although she doesn't have a mic she sings:

> *I never really cared for pleasure,*
> *So I smile when your words cut me like a razor.*
> *Deep pain, deep pain.*
> *The only thing that keeps me sane.*
> *Deep pain, deep pain.*
> *Please slice me again and again.*

And in the middle of it all, what she hopes for most is that Zak is filming this, so a little bit of what she is doing now will remain forever.

Chapter 40

The door of the tour bus slides closed with a sigh, and Zak and Linda are safely inside. They're getting a lift with the band. Linda is exhausted, but she still has the concert going round in her head, so there's no point trying to sleep. Nobody else looks particularly sleepy either. The bus moves off, saying a goodbye to the town and the concert hall. A poster for the Pet Monsters concert is peeling from a wall, and one of the corners is flapping. Linda feels like it's waving goodbye, but she knows it's only the wind.

She takes her phone out of her pocket. She forgot to answer her mother's text, and now she has a pile of missed calls. She doesn't even need to check who they're from.

'Oh my God, eighteen missed calls, and a text from Maria,' she groans.

'Oh, dear,' says Zak, leaning over to see what it says.

Your mum rang. Sorry. I couldn't lie well enough. :-(She went ballistic! Come home now!

'So, you didn't ask permission to come?'

'What do you think?'

Zak puts his arms around her comfortingly. Then he shows her the video of the concert. It looks very cool. The sound is a bit dodgy, but Linda does a pretty good job on the bass.

'Did you film it? Let's see,' says Tommy, grabbing the mobile to look. 'Wow, that's awesome! We've gotta put that on our blog!'

'Yeah, that's amazing,' agrees Chris. 'You've really gotta join a band, Linda!'

'But I can only play one song,' says Linda, her cheeks burning from all the attention.

'Well, I reckon you look like a real rock star,' says Tommy.

Tommy's last comment makes her cheeks burn even more. She's glad the bus is dark, so that nobody can see her face right now. Zak still has his arm around her. It feels safe, like having a big brother, and she leans her head on his chest. She can feel herself falling asleep.

'You're still coming with me, all the way?' she asks, her face buried in the black t-shirt.

'I certainly am!' says Zak.

It occurs to Linda again that Zak doesn't have a smell. But then, everything around her seems to be growing less and less distinct at the moment, not just smells.

The last thing she hears is Andreas telling them that they can take Linda and Zak as far as Voss, and then the band are heading west towards Bergen. Zak answers that Voss will be perfect, and that he's sure they'll get a lift from there with a lorry or something.

Linda is still tired and aching when they stop at the petrol station at Voss. Though that's hardly surprising as it's the middle of the night. Everybody, except Zak, is gobbling up hotdogs. The boys in the band wanted to buy Zak one too, but he said he was a veggie. Linda is leaning on a tall counter. She's got Tommy to herself for a bit, while the others wander about among the shelves, peering at the useful-to-have-in-the-car-things like ice scrapers, thermos cups with holders, sunglasses and lord-knows-what. Linda would like to have a proper, meaningful conversation with Tommy, but can't find the words. She barely dares look at him, and again she thinks how stupid she is to like him so much. But then, there's no law against liking someone. It's not as if she's seriously considering kissing him or something. She knows he's too old. It's Axel she's going to kiss, providing she and Zak get there before her parents stop her. Good God, kiss Tommy?! How ridiculous. It's enough to make her laugh! Which is what she suddenly does.

'What are you laughing at?' asks Tommy. 'Have I got ketchup all over my face?'

Linda peers over at him, and laughs even harder when she sees a blob of ketchup on his nose.

'Yes, you've got a bit there,' she says.

She wipes it off the tip of his nose with her serviette. She has no idea where she gets the courage.

'Ha-ha. Good job you're making sure I don't ruin my image! A rock star with ketchup on his nose. That's not cool!' he laughs.

'No,' she says, relieved that he's laughing.

Then, as though they'd read each other's minds, they race to see who can finish their hotdog and Coke the fastest. Linda wins and celebrates her victory by thumping her chest and releasing a big burp. Tommy looks at her in horror and then bursts into laughter and tries to do the same. But he fails to produce such an impressive burp. Linda giggles, pleased with herself.

'So, how did you get so famous?' she asks.

'The Pet Monsters aren't exactly famous,' he says, suddenly looking a bit embarrassed.

'Maybe not, but you've made records and you tour the whole country. You're living a dream,' she says.

'Yeah, that's what I used to think before we made our big breakthrough. But now it just seems kind of normal. We're the same guys as we were; a bunch of small-town boys who started playing together at high school. I don't feel as special as I thought I would,' he says.

'Can I tell you a secret?'

'If you want.'

'I'm going to die soon,' she says.

And as she says it she sees the same look come into his eyes, the same shadow of fear, as she's seen in the eyes of everyone else she's ever told. And then the sense of agitation she's noticed in their bodies, as though they were wearing an incredibly itchy jumper but had to hide their discomfort. But still, Linda decides to continue.

'That's why we're going to the south coast. I've got to put something right that I did wrong, before I die. I can't just sit at home and be frightened, while I wait for death to come and get me.'

'Well, that was some secret,' says Tommy. The agitation has

crept into his fingers, and he's picking at the label on his bottle.

'Usually I try to behave as though it's not true. Because everyone who knows I'm going to die gets so scared.'

Tommy stops picking. He swallows hard and looks up at her. But he can't hold her gaze.

'So what's down south?'

'There's a boy. He's called Axel,' says Linda.

It feels good to have mentioned Axel. That way Tommy won't suspect that she likes him as much as she does. Or, then again, maybe she's no better at controlling her body language than he is.

'Is that the boyfriend you were talking about? The guy who taught you to play the bass?' asks Tommy, throwing his empty bottle in the rubbish bin.

'Oy, there! Bottles go in the recycling!' comes an angry voice from behind the counter.

'Oops, sorry,' says Tommy, fishing the bottle back out of the bin. It looks like he's about to walk over to the bottle bank, and so Linda hurries on with her story.

'But I was lying when I said he was my boyfriend.'

'Why?'

'Because I want him to be my boyfriend. It was meant to be. Always. It's just that I didn't know until now. And this summer I was really mean to him, that's why I have to go to him now. I have to beg his forgiveness before I die.'

'That's one of the bravest things I've ever heard,' says Tommy.

'Thanks.'

Linda looks at Tommy again. He seems rather upset. She suddenly feels stupid for having poured out the whole story about her dying. She's been yelling at everyone not to remind her that she's going to die, and now here she is talking about it to someone she had no reason to tell. Somebody who could have seen her as a completely normal girl.

'We'd have offered you a lift all the way, but we can't. The tour goes on, and we've got to be in Bergen early tomorrow,' says Tommy, peering at his watch. 'Although strictly speaking it's tomorrow already!'

He laughs. Linda laughs back, and says it's not a problem. They're sure to get a lift from here.

'Take good care, then,' he says.

'I will,' says Linda.

'And you're welcome to play with us again some time.'

'Thank you. And thanks for the hotdog and Coke.'

Tommy just nods, before picking up the bottles and taking them over to the bottle bank. Then he winks at Linda as he walks back past her and out into the night, which will soon turn to morning.

Chapter 41

Zak is sitting on a crate outside the petrol station, leaning against the wall. Linda goes and sits next to him. He opens his eyes and smiles.

'Everything okay?'

'I suppose. Did you sleep?'

'Meditated. You're looking very thoughtful. What's up?'

'Oh, nothing . . . or, rather, I don't quite know yet. There won't be any buses from here at this time of night. But do you think we'll get a lift?'

'In five minutes,' says Zak, leaning back and closing his eyes again.

'How do you know that?'

'I don't know it, I just believe it,' says Zak smiling.

Linda feels quite awake now that she's eaten. She leans forward with her elbows resting on her knees and scans the horizon for cars. Soon a van turns into the petrol station forecourt, but it's only a guy delivering some stacks of newspapers. Linda barely manages to get to her feet before the van races off again.

'Relax,' says Zak, without opening his eyes.

She closes her eyes and tries to sit calmly like him. She counts to ten and then back to zero, trying to breathe in time with her counting and let her thoughts drift, the way Zak taught her on the train. But it's difficult, especially when she's feeling so cold. But she tries.

'What did I say?' says Zak suddenly, poking her.

A lorry has driven into the forecourt, and a little guy wearing heavy clogs and baggy jeans jumps down from the cab. He disappears into the petrol station and through the window they see him ordering a hotdog.

'Do you think he's going south?' asks Linda.

'Well, he was driving from the north,' says Zak.

With a hotdog in one hand, the morning paper under his arm and a Coke stuffed in his back pocket, the lorry driver comes back out of the shop.

'Hey! Joe!' shouts Linda, smiling as she walks towards him.

He stops, looking confused.

'If that's your name . . . I saw it up there on your lorry,' Linda says, pointing up at the sign that says Joe Nilsen.

The lorry driver looks up at his cab, before nodding and wiping his mouth with a serviette.

'You want something?'

'Are you driving south?'

'I'm driving home to Haugesund.'

'Is it possible to hitch a ride?'

'Aren't you a bit young to be hitch-hiking?' asks Joe, before stuffing the rest of his hotdog into his mouth.

'I'm with Zak. He's . . . my big brother,' says Linda, smiling as innocently as she can.

'Still, hitch-hiking can be dangerous. What if you took a ride with someone bad?'

Zak gets up from his crate. He goes over to Joe and offers him his hand.

'I'm Zak. Lucky for us, then, that we found a nice guy like you.'

'Right,' says Joe, shaking Zak's hand.

'You see, Joe, we're on the way to see our grandmother, and we've lost all our money. So it would be perfect if we could come with you.'

Zak's certainly a good liar, thinks Linda.

'Yes, and our parents are away in Spain, and since it's the first time they've been on holiday without us, we don't want to worry them by ringing them,' says Linda, hoping that Joe doesn't point out that it's the middle of the night.

'Well, as I was saying, I'm on my way home to Haugesund. You can come as far as that, at least.'

'Brilliant!' says Linda.

Joe unlocks the cab and opens the door on the passenger's side. Linda clambers in first and Zak follows. The driver's cab is covered with pictures of a woman with blonde hair. There's even a picture of her on the well-worn thermos cup on the dashboard. There's a picture on the calendar hanging next to the driver's seat too, but of a woman with even blonder hair, and with a massive smile and huge boobs. Dolly Parton, it says in pink letters. Linda picks up all the

CDs on the seat and puts them on the dashboard before sitting down. Joe opens the door on the driver's side, throws in the newspaper followed by the Coke bottle, and then climbs in.

'Who's Dolly Parton?' asks Linda.

'She's the queen of country,' says Joe, fastening his safety belt.

'I've never heard of her. Is she dead?'

'No, she's very much alive. Dolly Parton is a real classy lady, who sings about the most important thing in life,' says Joe.

'And what's that?'

'Love,' says Joe, putting on some music.

As they turn out of the petrol station forecourt, Joe breaks into song with a falsetto voice: 'I really got the feeling that I'll love you for a long, long time.' Linda nudges Zak and giggles quietly. But, if she's honest, Joe hasn't got such a bad voice, and Dolly Parton makes great motorway music. So Linda leans back and decides to enjoy the trip.

Linda must have fallen asleep again, because they're soon driving onto the ferry from Kvandal to Utne. Joe switches off the engine, and asks what happened to the newspaper he bought.

'I don't know,' says Linda.

'Here it is,' says Zak, passing it to him. 'I had a look at it. There's nothing interesting.'

'It's good to keep up with the news,' says Joe, spreading the newspaper out. 'Oh dear! War, murder, rising prices. You're right, there's nothing worth reading,' Joe says, shaking his head with a sigh, and folding the paper up again.

Linda leans forward to look at the back page with the weather chart.

'Well, at least it's going to be nice weather here today,' she says, pointing at it.

'Well I never!' says Joe. 'A day without rain in these parts. Now that's what I call good news!'

The ferry conductor bangs on the window and interrupts their philosophizing. Joe opens the lorry door. His pass pays for all three of them. Zak leans back in his seat and pretends to be asleep. But Linda feels awake again, and wants to talk. Dolly Parton is still singing 'I Will Always Love You' in the background, and her songs seem as perfect for the ferry ride as for a motorway drive.

'That's so lovely,' says Linda, turning up the volume.

Joe doesn't answer. He just let's the music play for a time.

Suddenly Joe leans forward and turns the CD player off.

'That's the saddest song I know,' he says, wiping his eyes.

'Why?'

'It reminds me of my Ingrid,' says Joe, choking back tears, and then covering it up by knocking back the rest of his Coke. 'Oh dear, I'd better go and buy a cup of coffee.'

'No, stay. Tell me about Ingrid instead. Is she the one in all the pictures?' asks Linda, resting a hand on Joe's arm in the hope of making him stay.

'Yes, that's Ingrid,' he says, putting the lid back on the empty plastic bottle. 'Ingrid is the finest woman in the world, after Dolly Parton. And she was my lady, until that Swedish rat stole her from me. Ludvig. A doctor. What chance did I have against a doctor? When I was just a miserable midwife.'

'Wow, are you really a midwife?'

'That's right. These hands have brought a thousand babies into this world. But after Ludvig came along and stole my Ingrid, I couldn't hack it any more. So I got a lorry-driver's permit, and now I'm a long-distance lorry driver.'

'But perhaps you'll meet someone else,' says Linda encouragingly.

'There's no woman like Ingrid,' says Joe, with a lump in his throat.

'Perhaps it would be easier to get over her if you took all these pictures down, and played some other music, instead of that sentimental country rubbish,' suggests Zak, who has suddenly come to life next to Linda.

'I don't know if I'll ever get over her,' says Joe.

'Hmm,' says Zak, leaning forward to switch the radio back on.

'. . . a thirteen-year-old girl has been reported missing . . .' Linda throws herself at the radio and changes the station.

'. . . *when the going gets tough, we'll dance through the night, and I'll hold you so tight, yeah, yeah, sweet baby, gotta live life* . . .'

'Listen, it's some rock. This will cheer you up,' says Linda.

The back gate of the ferry yawns open towards Utne. The

dawn light is creeping into the sky. And as the lorry drives off the ferry onto the quay, the song from the radio almost screams about living life to the full. Yes, thinks Linda to herself, that's exactly what I'm trying to do.

Chapter 42

Joe flashes his lights and honks his horn to say goodbye, as he turns his lorry out of the slip road by the motorway. Linda and Zak wave goodbye too. They are alone again, this time on a scarily deserted stretch of road. But it was better to jump out close to Aksdal rather than going all the way to Haugesund. Now that Linda's disappearance is being broadcast on the radio, it's best to stay away from any towns. It was lucky Joe didn't notice. Joe offered to drop them off in the middle of Aksdal, and they'd thanked him, but said no. They're too close to their goal to risk being stopped now. In fact they ought to be careful about hitch-hiking and taking buses too. Joe pointed out the direction they need to go.

'I suppose we'd better start walking,' says Zak, when Joe has turned the corner.

'This is a hopeless project,' Linda sighs. 'Besides, I'm shattered. Can't we find somewhere to sleep for a while?'

'Sure, but at least let's start to walk in the right direction. Come on, I'll give you a piggyback.'

'Are you sure you can manage?'

'Yes, for a while anyway. I'm stronger than I look.'

Linda jumps up onto his back, and he starts to walk. They'll never get there at this rate. She sighs, though she's decided not to moan.

'Something the matter?' asks Zak.

'No. It's not as cold as it was,' she says, trying to sound optimistic.

'Well, we're heading for the spring.'

'What a lovely thought,' says Linda, resting her cheek upon Zak's shoulder. 'We're heading for the spring.'

Linda closes her eyes and feels the sun warming her face. Not a lot, but it helps. Just as every step brings her a little closer to her goal.

Zak stops and lets Linda down from his back. They've come to a little farm that looks uninhabited. There's a red barn at the side of the road. Trustingly, it's been left open. The latch just has to be lifted, and anyone can walk in. So that's what they do. The air is dry and smells of hay, and there's just enough for a little bed. Linda walks over and lets herself collapse into it.

'Oh, how amazing,' she says.

'Are you cold?' asks Zak, kneeling down beside her. 'Let me tuck you in.'

He piles hay on top of her, so that she's lying cosily in a little nest.

'Thank you,' she says. 'And thank you for coming.'

'It's nothing. I had to come down south anyway,' he answers.

'Do you think we'll get there?'

'Of course,' he says.

'Will you guess when, again?'

'No, because we're so close. What could stop us?'

'I don't know. Maybe you're right.'

'I am right. Now stop worrying.'

'Aren't you going to take a little rest too?' asks Linda, realizing that she's more asleep than awake.

'No. I think I'll take a look around. Something might turn up that can get us there in the blink of an eye. What would be the most amazing thing that could happen now?'

'If we suddenly found a car,' says Linda, laughing. 'Will you hold my hand until I fall asleep?'

'Of course,' says Zak. He settles next to her and gives her his hand.

'Hey, you're so cold.'

'It's still February,' he says, giving her hand a gentle kiss.

Chapter 43

Linda dreams. The dream takes her back in time and to the south coast. The summer holidays are over, and the car has been packed for the return journey back up north to Trondheim. Axel has come to say goodbye. He is sitting on his bike with one foot on the pedal and the other on the ground. He lifts his hand to her face, and is about to say something. But just as he opens his mouth, Linda is sucked out of the picture. Her body is whisked forward in time, and suddenly she is on the wall of the Nidaros Cathedral. She is scrambling up it with her bare hands and feet. She is like a spider, and the wall is much higher than she remembered. When she looks down, a huge chasm opens up below her. It is filled with flames and smoke. She hears screams and realizes that it's hell. If she loses her foothold now she'll be doomed. The thought barely enters her mind when she slips and falls. But somebody grabs her. It is Zak. He looks deep into her eyes. Linda can see the flames of hell reflected in his pupils, as he drags her to safety. Then her body is sucked back to the scene with Axel, and she's sitting in the car again. But this time the car is already driving away. She sees her hand pressed up against the back window, and hears herself whisper: I'll miss you too.

Words that have been said too late to be heard. She turns to face forwards, and sees the backs of her parents' heads. They are sitting in the front, talking to each other. Linda feels somehow that they're not sitting in the same car. And perhaps they aren't. She opens the back passenger door and steps out of the car while it's moving. Her parents don't even notice. The car just drives on with the back door swinging. They don't even seem to have noticed. They just race off to get to the ferry on time. They reach the ferry, and only as it leaves the quayside with them on board do they see that the back seat of the car is empty. Her mother screams. Screams, and tears open the door. Stumbles across the deck and runs to the stern. But however loud she screams, however hard she grabs the ticket man and shouts that they can't just leave their daughter behind, the ferry does not turn back. Then blood starts to flow from under her mother's summer dress. Streams of blood run down her thighs and calves. She grabs her stomach.

Linda wakes up sobbing. Zak is sitting there watching her.

'Good morning,' he says.

'I had such a sad dream,' says Linda, wiping her face.

'About what?'

'About Mum and Dad. We were on our way home from holiday. They thought I was in the back of the car. But I wasn't. Mum just screamed and screamed, and then she started bleeding. It's the second time I've dreamed of her losing the baby. Do you think it means something? Will it be my fault if they lose this baby?'

'Perhaps your dream just means you miss them?' Zak suggests.

'I think perhaps I was wrong to go. They've reported me missing, and all I've done is switch off my phone. They must be scared. Perhaps the dream is telling me that I'm making Mum so scared that she'll lose the baby.'

'She's not going to lose the baby. You're going to get your little brother this time, I promise.'

'How can you possibly promise that? You're not an angel, after all, are you?' Linda protests.

'Do you think it's up to angels to fix the world?'

Linda doesn't answer. She just shakes her head, even though she'd love to think angels existed, and that they could fix everything, and that Zak was one of them.

'Do you want to turn back?'

'No. No. The strange thing is that I feel so much stronger. My heart hasn't acted weird since we left Trondheim.'

'I'm glad you feel better. You look better too. But perhaps you should ring your parents, so your conscience feels a little lighter too?'

'Okay. Will you wait for me outside while I talk to them?'

'Of course.'

He strokes her cheek with the back of his hand, almost as though she was just a little child and he was very, very old. Linda waits until Zak has left before taking out her phone.

She turns it on and keys in the pin code. A flood of texts appears. Linda can't be bothered to start reading them all. Instead she just dials her home number. Her parents must be sitting right by the phone, because they answer straight away.

'Hi, it's me,' she says.

'Linda, what are you doing? Where are you?' her mother yells down the line.

There's no way she can hide the fact she's hysterical. Not that Linda thinks she's exactly trying.

'I'll be back soon. Don't worry, Mum. There's just something I have to do,' says Linda.

'There's only one thing you have to do now, and that's get yourself back home!' bellows her father, who has taken the receiver.

'I'm sorry, but I can't.'

'Can't or won't?' he yells.

'Both,' she says.

She can hear that her mum has taken the receiver again. She can hear her sobbing and gearing up to say something else. Linda can't bare to listen to any more. They don't understand. They don't understand and she can't cope with it. She ends the call, and then switches off the telephone completely. Then she gets up. She brushes away a few strands of hay and weighs the mobile in her hand, before letting it drop to the ground. Then she kicks it into the darkest corner of the barn and leaves. Zak is sitting outside, leaning against a sunny wall with his eyes closed. She goes over to him and stands in front of him, casting a shadow over him. He opens his eyes.

'Did it go alright?'

'Yes. No problem. They just wished us a good trip,' says Linda.

Chapter 44

'You'll never guess what I've found,' says Zak, laughing.

'What?'

'Come with me and I'll show you,' he says.

He stretches out a hand. Linda takes it and pulls him up to his feet.

'I investigated the rest of the farm while you were asleep.'

Zak leads Linda to an old stable. He lifts the latch and pushes the door open. Linda can see something pretty big under tarpaulin. A tractor perhaps?

'This,' says Zak, 'is precisely what we need.'

He lifts a corner of the tarpaulin, so Linda can see a car. A rather clapped-out old banger, but a car nevertheless. Zak pulls back the cover, releasing a shower of dust and dirt, and throws it into a corner.

'It may not look smart, but I've already tried to start it and it goes like clockwork,' he boasts, getting in. 'Come on, jump in!'

Linda gets in. She notices that Zak isn't using an ignition

key like any normal person. Instead he's fiddling with some wires. It all looks far from legal.

'Are we stealing this car?'

'Hmm. It's a kind of loan,' says Zak, his face lighting up as the motor starts up. 'What did I say? Works like a dream!'

'Have you asked if you can borrow it? And if so, where's the ignition key?'

'Well, I haven't exactly asked, but the owner doesn't use it any more. Look, it's covered with dust,' he says, blowing the dashboard so that a cloud of dust fills the air.

'Zak, when we were in the cathedral, you said we should be aware of our inner compass, and of the things we do wrong . . .'

'Well, yes. Because then we can ask for forgiveness afterwards,' says Zak, with a grin.

'Isn't it best to avoid doing things we have to ask forgiveness for afterwards? We can't just take this car.'

'Do you want to go and see Axel or not?' he asks.

Zak stalls the car and it lurches forward.

'Do you even know how to drive?'

'La-di-da, la-di-da,' says Zak, getting out of the car and slamming the door after him. 'As you want. We'll go and ask if we can borrow it.'

'Or we could take the bus,' says Linda, slinking out of the car too.

'The owner probably lives up there in that house,' says Zak, pointing up the hill, and stomping towards it. Linda hangs back. They might just as well take the bus from here. It's unlikely anyone will recognize her with her new blue hair.

And they're very close now anyway. She thinks about her parents and how frantic they were. They hadn't listened to her at all. She just hopes they don't discover where she's going and try to stop her. It's a good job she got rid of her phone. Linda kicks a stone. She follows it with her gaze. It lands in the middle of something green and white that's peeping through last year's yellow grass.

'Snowdrops. There are snowdrops over here,' she shouts.

Zak turns and puts his hands on his hips. But Linda pretends not to see how exasperated he is and walks over to the flowers and starts picking them. 'It's good to bring a gift when you're going to ask to borrow a car.'

'Yeah, sure. And it's even better when it's a bunch of flowers you found in the owner's garden! You're the one who was talking so piously about right and wrong a minute ago!'

Linda doesn't answer. She carries on until she's got a bunch, and then goes over to Zak who's standing there waiting. He rolls his eyes and then strides off again. Linda looks up at the house. A head pokes round the kitchen curtains. They are being observed. What's the worst that can happen? Linda thinks to herself.

'That she tells you off for picking her snowdrops,' says Zak, answering her thoughts.

'How did you know . . . ?'

'Well, she's standing up there, glaring out of her window. Come on,' he says, laughing.

When they get to the house, he leaps up the front steps and rings the bell. Then he runs back and pushes Linda forward, before withdrawing into the background.

'Hey, that's not fair—' says Linda.

She is interrupted by the door opening.

'I'm not interested in buying lottery tickets,' says an elderly lady at the door.

'That's lucky. We're not selling any,' answers Linda.

'So what are you after then?'

'Er, we're doing a school project about the old days, and we wondered if we could interview you?'

'I don't remember a single thing,' says the woman.

Linda pretends not to have heard this last comment. She just walks up the front steps, holding out the flowers.

'Are those for me?'

'Yes.'

The woman hesitates then takes the little bouquet. She sniffs it before fixing Linda with her gaze.

'Hmm. I saw you picking them down there in my garden.'

'I'm sorry,' says Linda.

A smile spreads over the old lady's face as she lets the door swing open and disappears into a dark hallway.

'Well, you'd better come in. Don't bother to take your shoes off. The home help's coming today and she needs something to do, the lazy creature.'

Chapter 45

Zak and Linda are now safely planted on Olga's sofa. It's hard to decide whether Olga is a cantankerous old biddy, or just has a unique sense of humour. The living room smells of stewed prunes and biscuits, and the clock ticks loudly.

'Just tuck in,' she says, shoving a cake towards them. It's of the shop-bought-with-a-scarily-long-sell-by-date variety.

Linda shakes her head. She's already had two whole sand-wiches and a big glass of milk. Zak gets up and paces around the room. Linda knows why; the radio is on and the news is blaring out. Then it comes: a thirteen year old girl from Trondheim has been reported missing. Police do not believe there to be any criminal involvement, but people are asked to . . .' Zak turns off the radio.

'Excuse me! Why did you do that? The weather forecast will be on soon,' Olga protests.

'Overcast with the possibility of a little rain later this evening. But I can't see it'll make any difference. You surely weren't thinking of going out?' says Zak.

'No, but it's good to follow things,' says Olga, clearly offended, and taking a piece of cake herself.

'I like your house,' says Linda, trying to avoid any argument. What's going on with Zak? He seems to be getting increasingly rude and childish. And right now, when they want to borrow the car and everything!

'So, you're here to interview elderly folk. A kind of school project, you said? The old days, indeed! You youngsters should be more concerned with the future!' says Olga, taking a bite of her cake.

'Well yes, but . . .'

Linda starts to clear the plates and glasses; hers dirty, Zak's unused. She gets up to put them in the kitchen.

'You don't need to tidy up. The home help is coming today.'

'But it won't take a minute.'

Linda signals to Zak that he should follow her out. In the kitchen she grabs his arm.

'What are we going to do now?' she asks.

'I don't know. This was your idea!'

'My idea? Hardly! I wanted to take the bus.'

'There are radios on buses, and on the radio there's news, and today you're news, or have you forgotten that?'

'Thanks for nothing,' Linda says, turning on her heel.

What is it with Zak right now? He's suddenly so childish. It's as though he can't be bothered to help her. She pauses at the doorway to the living room, waiting for Zak to say something. Anything. But he is silent. She turns to him, and he's just standing there gawping. Okay, she'll have to deal with this herself somehow. She takes a deep breath and goes into the living room. Olga looks up, before continuing to scrape her plate with her fork. Linda smiles mechanically and crosses the room, past the noisy clock, over to the old piano, on which some photographs are displayed. She leans forward and peers at a picture of a younger Olga standing next to a man in front of a car. It's the car that Zak found in the barn.

'Can I take this picture down to look at it more closely?' asks Linda.

'With pleasure,' says Olga, putting down her plate.

Linda takes the picture over to the sofa and passes it to Olga, who takes it in both hands. She looks at it and smiles, before wiping some dust off the frame with her sleeve.

'That's Karl and me on a car trip. Karl loved that car. He spent more time tinkering with that car than he spent with me!' says Olga, laughing.

'Were you jealous of the car?' asks Linda.

'Oh no! That was just something we joked about. We had so many lovely trips together. We're in Balestrand in this picture. We stayed in a lovely hotel, overlooking the fjord. We had plenty of time on our hands, you see, when the children had flown the nest.'

Olga pauses and gazes at the picture. Then she rubs it again with her sleeve, to remove some invisible dust from the man's face. Then she traces her fingers over the car.

'I didn't have the heart to get rid of the car after he died. My kids say I'm a sentimental old fool,' says Olga, with a little laugh.

'Is that because you loved Karl so much?' asks Linda, hesitantly.

'Mmm,' says Olga, pausing. Linda can see Olga's eyes are moist. 'I still love him. Love is stronger than death, you know. Karl lives as strongly in my heart as he ever did. We were meant to be, right from the start. Karl said he fell in love with me when he was just a lad. His father was doing a carpentry job at the farm where I lived, and Karl came along too. Our cat had just had kittens, and my mother told me to show them to the little boy who was visiting. Karl told me later that he'd decided there and then that he would marry the little girl with the long red plaits. We both grew up, and as youngsters we'd go to dances. I liked to dance and flirt with the other boys, but Karl was always the one who walked me home. And, just as he decided as a little boy, I became his wife, and we got our lovely bunch of children too.'

Olga smiles at the picture in her lap. Then she hands it to Linda, who walks over and puts it back on top of the piano.

For a moment Linda stands with her back to Olga.

'I told you a lie,' she says, with her gaze still fixed on the picture. 'We're not doing a school project at all. I was on my way to see a boy called Axel. We've known each other forever. And last summer I did something really stupid.'

Linda closes her eyes. Not that it helps to close them, since what she's seeing is inside her head. She sees herself in Axel's room, sitting in there alone. She gets up from the bed and goes over to the desk. She opens the drawer. It's the drawer where Axel hid the notebook that he hadn't wanted her to see. And even though she knows it's wrong, she takes the notebook out. She sits down at his desk and reads it. It is full of poems:

> *There's a girl I know who glides through the sea.*
> *Like a dolphin she darts, bringing summer to me.*
> *Soon she'll be here, in my heart I feel sure.*
> *I hope and I wonder, are we friends or more?*

Linda leafs on, and finds another poem.

'What are you doing?' says Axel.

Linda freezes. She hadn't heard him come in.

'Do you write poems?' she says.

She can hear that her voice is so harsh that it sounds like an attack.

'Give me that book,' says Axel.

'No,' says Linda, reading aloud from it sarcastically:

> *Cowboys and Indians was the game we'd play,*
> *And we played together every day . . .*

Axel walks towards her. But Linda is quick, and climbs up onto the desk and reads on scornfully:

> *It was always summer when you were near,*
> *In the winter the snow came, and . . .*

Linda stops. She's frightened that he'll grab her and pull her down from the desk. Her stomach is churning madly. But he doesn't move. He just stands there and looks up at her.

'Do you think I'm daft for writing poetry?'

She hasn't got an answer. So she just laughs. And then laughs some more, to cover up the horrible feelings of shame she feels inside.

'I thought I could trust you,' says Axel, as he walks away.

'Well, my dear,' says Olga, rescuing Linda from her embarrassing memory. 'We all do things we regret.'

'And that's why we came. We need your car,' says Linda, pointing at the car in the picture, with her gaze fixed on Olga. 'We've got to get to the south coast quickly. I have to see Axel. A few weeks ago I found out that I might not live as long as I thought, so I don't have much time.'

'Are you hoping Axel will be your sweetheart?'

'Yes. I think he will be. And it would be such a great help if you could—'

'Do we get the car or not?' Zak interrupts.

Linda looks at him. Oh my God! He's probably ruined everything now!

Chapter 46

It is late afternoon and beginning to get dark. Zak and Linda are now driving along in their own car, and fast approaching their goal. Zak's outrageous cheek had resulted in Olga fetching the car keys. And then he'd laughed disdainfully all the way back to the barn: as if he didn't know how to hotwire a car!

'How did you learn to drive a car?' asks Linda.

Zak doesn't answer. He just swings into an open space, puts the car in neutral and pulls on the handbrake.

'What are you doing?' asks Linda.

'I'm not doing anything . . . you are,' he says.

He gets out of the car, and leaving his door open runs to the passenger side.

'Come on out,' he says, opening her door.

Linda gets out, and Zak sits in the passenger seat. As she stands hesitating, he rolls the window down.

'Do you want to get there, or what?'

'Well, yes.'

'Well, get a move on. We can't leave the engine running.

Think about the environment,' he says sarcastically, winding the window back up.

'Alright,' Linda says, mostly to herself.

She walks round the car and sits behind the wheel.

Zak helps her to adjust the mirror. Then he shows her the brakes and the clutch and the accelerator.

'We're in neutral now,' he explains. 'To start driving you have to press your foot down on the clutch, put the car in first gear, put your foot on the brake, then take off the handbrake and gently press on the accelerator.'

Linda follows his instructions. The car lurches forward and stalls.

'Try again. On with the handbrake, in with the clutch, turn the ignition, foot gently down on the accelerator, and now take off the handbrake, and bring your foot off the clutch – slowly.'

This time the car starts rolling. Not fast, but she's driving! Oh my God! She's got butterflies in her stomach. Zak says she should move into the next gear. And that goes like a dream too.

'I'm driving!' she says, looking at Zak.

'You certainly are,' he says, turning on the radio.

'Now try to move into third gear,' he shouts through the music.

Linda obeys. Driving is easy. It's going brilliantly. A car comes towards them, and Zak brings his hand up to the wheel and helps her steer.

'You have to fix your gaze on the approaching car, then you'll steer better. *Yeah, yeah, sweet baby, gotta live life!*' sings Zak.

'It so strange that they keep playing that song on the radio,' says Linda, turning towards Zak.

Suddenly the car swerves towards a ditch. Zak grabs the wheel and helps her to pull the car back straight.

'You mustn't turn the car and your head at the same time,' laughs Zak.

He suddenly grows very serious.

'Turn into that road into the forest,' he says.

'Which road?' she asks.

'That one.'

This time he grabs the wheel with both hands and turns it so violently that, in spite of the loud music, Linda can hear the wheels screech. There's a smell of burned rubber. Stones hit the belly of the car, and it shudders. Linda screams and shuts her eyes. Instinctively she lifts her feet, bringing her knees up and protecting her head with her arms. Despite the seatbelt digging into her right shoulder, she is thrown into the wheel and then back into her seat. She brings her hand to her nose, and feels warm blood running through her fingers. It's trickling down into her mouth too. She's in such pain, she can't even scream. There are stars in front of her eyes. It's silent, after the crash, apart from the wheezing of the engine. And as the stars in front of her eyes begin to disappear, she looks straight into Zak's face.

'Damn!' he whispers.

'Ow,' she whimpers.

'Are you mad?' he yells. 'You can't just take your feet off the pedals like that!'

'I'm sorry,' says Linda, on the edge of tears.

When she sees that they've crashed into the trunk of a tree, the tears start rolling down her face. There's smoke coming from the bonnet, which is completely smashed.

'We could have died,' Linda says, and as the words come out of her mouth the bonnet flies open, making her jump.

'Stop whining, you stupid little girl!' Zak yells.

Linda gets the urge to whack him over the head, as he leans forward to open the glove compartment. He is totally callous and vile. She's the one with the injuries. He hasn't got a scratch on him. Besides, he was the one that grabbed the wheel and turned it. It's as much his fault. Zak rummages around. He finds a pair of sunglasses and a roll of tissue paper. He takes them and gets out of the car, slamming the door so Linda jumps again. She tries to wipe the tears and blood away with her sleeve. Zak kicks one of the tyres and stares at the bonnet. He shakes his head. Then he walks around and opens the door on the driver's side. He leans in and undoes Linda's seatbelt, before grabbing her legs and swinging them out of the car.

'Are you alright?' he asks gently.

He tears off some tissue paper and carefully wipes the area around Linda's nose.

'Thanks,' she says.

Zak doesn't answer. He just strokes her cheek. Then he twists a little bit of tissue into a point, and very carefully pokes it up her nostril.

'Relax completely,' he says, putting a hand on either side of the bridge of her nose.

'What happening?' she says, feeling frightened.

'Shh. Just relax,' he says, looking deep into her eyes.

Suddenly Linda can feel his gaze making her very calm. So calm that she barely shudders when he wrenches her nose so hard it cracks.

'It was a bit crooked, but now it's straight again,' he says.

Zak takes one hand away from her nose, but let's the other rest there. Linda closes her eyes. A soft warmth replaces the pain.

'What . . . ?'

'Just sit calmly,' says Zak, placing his free hand in hers. 'It'll be alright.'

'Okay,' she whispers.

'There now,' he says, giving her hand a squeeze,

She feels herself getting sleepy. Zak puts her in the front seat of the car and adjusts it to a lying position.

'You just rest, Linda, and I'll watch over you,' he says.

Linda has barely closed her eyes before Zak shakes her and says that she's got to get out of the car.

'What? Why?' she says, looking round.

Linda lifts her hand to her nose. Amazingly it only feels a bit sore. She sits up and tries to look at herself in the driver's mirror, but it's too dark. She fumbles in the car roof for the light switch, but nothing happens when she presses it.

'How do I look?' she asks.

'Here, put these on,' says Zak, handing her the sunglasses he found in the glove compartment.

'Do I look that bad?'

'No worse than usual,' Zak jokes. 'I hope you've got enough money for the bus,' he says, suddenly bounding up to the main road and starting to wave his arms. At first, Linda just sees two lights. Then she sees a bus coming round the corner. It's driving so fast, she's scared Zak will get run over. But it swerves into the opposite lane and stops.

'Come on,' Zak shouts.

'But my bag,' Linda shouts back.

'Forget the stupid bag,' yells Zak.

Linda doesn't want to go without her bag. She packed it with lots of useful things for the trip. She flings the back door of the car open and grabs it before running up to the road. She arrives just in time to find the bus driver shouting at Zak.

'What the hell are you doing? You can't stand in the middle of the road like that!'

'I'm sorry, but it was an emergency,' says Zak. 'We've had a car crash and we need a lift.'

'A good thrashing, that's what you need. But you'd better jump in.'

'Thanks. My sister will pay,' says Zak, going to the back of the bus and sitting down.

Linda rummages for her purse in her bag. She can't see anything with these dark glasses on. But she doesn't dare take them off, since she doesn't know how bad she looks from the crash.

'Just go and sit down. You can pay at the next stop. We can't stand here in the middle of the road,' says the driver.

'Okay,' says Linda, surprised that the driver doesn't seem to have noticed anything unusual.

She moves to the back of the bus to join Zak. He is resting his head against the window with his eyes closed. Linda takes off the sunglasses cautiously, so she can see better. She opens her rucksack and finds a pocket mirror in her make-up case. Steeling herself, she flips the mirror open. She gasps. Her face looks completely fine! Her reflection gives her goosebumps. What did Zak do to her? She's about to poke him and ask, when she sees that they're driving past a couple of policemen that have pulled over a car. They seem to be writing out a speeding ticket or something.

'Oh my God,' she exclaims, feeling her heart gallop inside her chest.

'What?' says Zak, opening his eyes.

'We just drove straight past a police checkpoint.'

'Really?' says Zak, peering over his shoulder. 'Wow. That was lucky! We could have been stopped for driving too fast – or, even worse, too fast and with no licence.'

He gives a short giggle and then rests his head against the window and closes his eyes again.

'Did you know?'

'Know what?'

'That the police were there?' says Linda.

'How would I know that?' answers Zak, without opening his eyes.

Linda thinks she sees the corner of his mouth tremble. Yes, how could he possibly have known? Why has their journey been a series of so many lucky coincidences? Is there something she should have understood by now?

Chapter 47

Zak and Linda took another bus on from Stavanger and finally reached the summer cottage late in the evening. Nobody recognized Linda or suspected she might be the missing girl, because of her new blue hair and spiky cut. Zak insisted on coming with her beyond Stavanger. He made some excuse about wanting see where she spent her summers. He has avoided discussing his sister again, even though Linda has asked several times. Another subject he carefully avoids is what he did to her after the accident. There's a bit of a yellow-and-blue patch around Linda's nose, but by rights it should look much worse. Zak brushes her question off, saying it was because he'd wrenched her nose back into place so quickly. But he's been pretty grouchy and irritable most of the day. It's as though the confident, laid-back guy she met back in Trondheim, the guy with a philosophical answer for everything, has gone.

'You seem uptight. Is it something to do with your sister?' she asks gently.

'Stop asking!' Zak snarls.

'Oh, sorry for caring! You didn't have to come with me all the way, especially if you're just going to be grumpy,' Linda snarls back, stopping at the cottage gate.

'I want to see your cottage and this amazing guy Axel,' says Zak, pushing past her to open the gate.

'But what about your sister? Do I get to meet her?'

'Stop going on about her, will you?' he says, slamming the gate behind him and striding towards the cottage.

Linda opens the gate again and follows him up the winding path. He stands by the front door, peering in through a window. He has his hands around his eyes like a funnel, to see in better.

'Key?' he asks, turning towards her as she approaches. Any sign of his outburst down by the gate has gone.

'In my rucksack. The one you were so keen for me to leave in the car,' says Linda sarcastically, slipping it off her shoulder.

'We'd have got in without it,' says Zak, starting to whistle.

'We'd have broken in, would we? What happened to all that talk about right and wrong?'

'It's not exactly breaking in when it's your own cottage,' he says, standing aside.

Linda doesn't answer. She just turns the key in the lock and opens the door. The smell of twelve summers and a thousand memories rushes towards her from the hallway: the warm, musty odour of old raincoats, wellies and pine. She goes in and turns on the light.

'Come in, then,' she says over her shoulder.

Zak steps over the threshold and kicks off his boots, one of them with such force that it flies into the wall with a thud.

'Sorry,' he says, picking up both boots and putting them neatly on the doormat.

'Do you want a pair of socks?' asks Linda, passing him the basket of thick woollen socks that her family wear as slippers in the cottage.

'No, thanks,' says Zak.

Linda follows his gaze down to his socks and sees he has a hole in one of his big toes.

'Well, maybe,' he says, choosing a pair of grey rag-socks.

Linda takes her rainbow socks as usual. But as she pulls them on, she remembers they were a bit small for her last summer.

'That's strange,' she says, finding that they don't feel tight. Is her memory playing tricks?

'Well, are you going to show me around?' he says.

'Of course.'

Linda opens the door onto the large room, the kitchen and living room. She walks over to the large windows that face the sea and pulls back the curtains.

'Wow,' exclaims Zak.

'Yes. Amazing, isn't it?'

The view is so familiar to her, but she tries to see it through Zak's eyes now. The moon, which seems as full as on the night they were in the cathedral tower, lights up the landscape softly and glitters on the fjord.

'It must be amazing here in the summer,' he says.

'Yes. You see that rock over there? The huge one that drops straight down into the sea?'

'Yes?'

'We call it the Black Cliff, and every summer all the toughest teenagers dive from it. I've always thought I'd do it one day. Now I'll never know what it's like to do a dive like that.'

'Are you sure?' asks Zak, taking her hand.

'Doctor's orders.'

'Are you sure the doctor's right? You've been doing all sorts of things you shouldn't. You've climbed up the wall of Nidaros Cathedral, you've driven a car and crashed it. One more bad thing can't do you any harm, surely?' says Zak.

Linda wants to be persuaded by his argument.

She turns to Zak, who is standing close at her side and holding her hand. His face looks white in the light of the moon. White and almost luminous, but with dark-blue shadows under his eyes. He must surely be an angel, she thinks. What else can he be? Although she didn't know angels could be so grumpy. Suddenly Linda remembers a prayer her grandmother used to say when she went to stay the night in her downstairs flat: Now I lay me down to sleep, I pray the Lord my soul to keep. Isn't that what Zak has done this whole time? Taken care of her and lead her safely here? Yes, she wants to believe that. She wants to believe that everything is somehow linked.

So there she stands, on the edge of the Black Cliff. Her bare feet against the bare rock. She is shivering, in just her knickers and t-shirt. The moon has hidden itself behind the clouds, and the fjord is black beneath her. Which is just as well, since it makes it look less far down. She curls her toes, but that doesn't make her any warmer. She might just as well dive straight in. Standing here only makes it worse. Then it begins to snow. The flakes feel like little kisses against her skin, giving her goosebumps. She sees the hair on her arms rise. Zak is sitting on the jetty, waiting for her with a towel and a thick blanket. Linda tries to calm herself. She tells herself it isn't dangerous. The trick is to do the dive in exactly the same way as she would at the pool. Just keep calm. She can hear her coach's voice in her head. All the things he says when they're doing something more advanced: concentrate, focus, feel your body, run through the dive in your head, and remember to enter the water at the right angle. Not too steep an angle, nor too shallow. Linda stares down into the darkness. She hears the waves lapping against the rock below. Soon she'll be warm and safe again. Linda closes her eyes.

'If I survive this, I can survive anything,' she says to herself, lifting her arms above her head.

She tenses her body, and tries to feel her heart. It's beating a little faster than usual, but it doesn't feel bad. She looks down towards the jetty, and can just make out the shadowy form of Zak. Is he nodding? She can't tell.

Now she dives.

Chapter 48

They say your life flashes before your eyes when you're about to die. If that's the case, Linda is not going to die now. As she dives, and as she glides soundlessly into the icy water, she only sees pictures of a possible future. She sees Axel opening the door for her, smiling, inviting her in and kissing her. She sees herself as an older sister, holding a little bundle in her arms, and her parents beaming at her. She sees herself as a young woman, in a big lecture hall, writing important notes. She sees herself getting a job and a house of her own. She sees herself getting married to Axel, having children and getting old together. And at the end, at the very end, she sees an old woman sitting on a bench. And she knows that this old woman is herself. Linda stretches out and touches the woman's shoulder. The old woman turns and, lifting her hand to her head, she suddenly rips off her hair. It isn't an old version of herself who is laughing at Linda now, but Zak. Zak has thrown off the grey wig and is laughing at her. Linda opens her eyes. The water is pitch black all around her. She must swim back up. She struggles a little before she finally feels herself rising to the top. But instead of breaking the surface as she'd expected, she feels a hand on her head. A hand that's clutching at her hair and holding her under the water. She tries to wrench herself free. She grabs the hand and tugs at it. Bubbles stream from her mouth as she tries to scream underwater. She needs air. She needs air now! Is it Zak who's holding her down? It's impossible to get away, however hard she twists and turns. Then she tries a new tactic, making herself as heavy and lifeless as she can. She breathes out the last air in her lungs, to make herself sink better. Finally, the grip on her hair loosens, and she floats downwards, feeling warm, and weightless. Linda opens her eyes. She sees a gigantic cod swimming towards her. As it passes it strokes her face and slaps her with its tail. Linda starts to struggle towards the surface again. This time she gets her head above water, and gasps greedily for air. Then, desperate, she starts turning in the water, trying to get her bearings. She spots Zak sitting on the jetty. He is drying his arm, and pulling the sleeve of his coat back down. He is not even trying to disguise the fact that he was the one holding her head under the water. Linda feels a dark and violent anger rising in her.

'Oy, you!' she yells, swimming towards the jetty with long, strong strokes.

'Oh, hi there!' he says, folding the towel up neatly and putting it next to him. Then he stretches his hand out to help her up. Linda pretends not to have seen it, and climbs out on her own and grabs the towel. Without a word she pats herself dry, and Zak hands her the blanket.

'Well, that went perfectly!' says Zak, as if everything was normal.

'Perfectly? Perfectly! You tried to murder me!' Linda shouts.

'Don't exaggerate,' says Zak casually, arranging her shoes for her, so she can just shove her feet in.

Linda kicks them away and launches herself at Zak and pins him down on the jetty.

'Who are you . . . really?'

'Let me go,' says Zak calmly, sweeping her firmly to one side.

'What are you? What kind of sick being are you?' she asks, determined not to let him avoid the question this time. She's not giving up until she has an answer.

'This isn't exactly easy for me either, if that's what you think!' he yells.

Linda can see Zak's chest heaving up and down under his t-shirt.

'Damn! I think I need some time to myself,' he says, shaking his head angrily and walking off.

'No! No! No!' Linda shouts.

She throws herself at him and catches hold of one of his legs. But again he shakes her off, this time so violently that she rolls back out into the water. She struggles to the surface once again, only to find that the jetty is empty. She can see no sign of Zak.

'Damn you! To hell with you, you coward!' she screams into the night, hoping he can hear.

Then she turns onto her back in the water, and lies there, floating. Suddenly she feels her chest thumping wildly. There are too many things now that don't make sense. Why doesn't she feel the cold any more?

'Mum?' she hears herself say. And she sounds like a scared little girl. 'Mum?' she says again, as she swims back to the jetty, where she dries herself, and stuffs her feet in her shoes, without bothering to get dressed.

As she darts back up to the cottage with the blanket wrapped round her, she holds a hand to her chest. Her heart feels almost still, even though it's a steep path up from the water's edge. Linda feels someone following her in the dark. She glances round, but she can see no one. She gets a shudder up her spine. Is it Zak? Has he come back to kill her? The sound of meowing makes Linda sigh with relief. It's just a cat. She stops. The cat stops.

'Come on, pussycat,' says Linda, aware she needs company now.

The cat is completely black and reminds her of the cat she saw in her backyard at home. But it's difficult to distinguish one black cat from another. This one seems a lot friendlier than the last, as it trots after her. When she opens the door, it saunters confidently into the hallway. Linda can't help smiling, and the cat answers her with a purr.

'Do you want some food, my little friend?' she asks, looking down at the cat now rubbing itself against her legs. The feeling of its fur against her bare skin gives her goosebumps.

'I've got a sandwich in my bag. Do you want that?'

Linda gets the rest of her packed lunch out. Olga hadn't let them go without giving them some food for the journey. There are two sandwiches left, and a slab of that cake with the suspiciously distant sell-by date. The cat won't want that of course. Linda puts half a liver-pâté sandwich on the floor. The cat sniffs it, sticks its tail in the air and struts into the sitting room.

'Alright. So you're not hungry,' says Linda.

She thinks, rather than actually feels, that she needs a warm shower and dry clothes. The cat will have to look after itself for a while. She turns towards the front door and puts her hand on the lock. Should she put it on? Shouldn't she leave it open in case Zak returns? In case he regrets going off? Or perhaps the thought of his return ought to make her more determined to lock up. The way he held her under the water! She puts the lock on and goes into the bathroom. Linda looks in the mirror over the sink. Her nose looks perfectly fine, and even the tinge of yellowy blue has gone. It's hardly surprising she thought Zak was an angel, when he could cure her so quickly. It was like a miracle. Now she doesn't know what to think. Perhaps he's the opposite of an angel. A devil sent from hell to make her life unbearable.

Warm and dry, Linda lies on the sheepskin rug in front of the hearth. The fire crackles cosily. There's a stormy wind outside and it has started to rain. Even with the cat curled up and purring next to her, she feels lonely. She regrets throwing her mobile away. There's no phone at the cottage, and she'd love to hear her parents' voices right now. Even though they're bound to be angry and frightened. It would be nice to talk to Maria too, and tell her about the concert. She forgot to text the photo to Maria, and the film clip of her playing with the

Pet Monsters has gone now as well. How could she be so stupid to have thrown her phone away? Surely it would have been enough just to switch it off? And perhaps she should have rung Axel, or at least sent him a text? Imagine if he's not at home when she rings at his door tomorrow? Oh well, she won't see that phone again. Linda lies on her back, closes her eyes and tries to sleep. The cat is lying right next to her ear, purring. Linda sighs, and shuts her eyes even tighter. No more brooding now, she's got to sleep.

Chapter 49

Linda is woken by the daylight in her room. The fire has gone out in the hearth, but it's still nice and warm. Sleepily, she stretches out under the duvet. Suddenly, there's a knock at the door. Linda sits up. Zak? Should she open it? Before she has time to decide, she hears the lock being turned from outside. Is he picking the lock? Linda is on her feet in a flash. She dashes out into the hallway, and nearly collides with her mother.

'Mum?'

'So this is where you are!' says her mother, her voice slipping uncontrollably into a falsetto.

Her father appears immediately behind. He hangs up his keys on the hook where Linda's are already hanging.

'What have you done to yourself?' asks her mother, touching Linda's new blue hairdo.

'I got it cut,' answers Linda, taking her mother's hand to stop her. Right now, she's very glad Zak fixed her nose so well. Even if it was kind of brutal the way he did it.

Linda and her mother stand looking at each other. Linda is

still holding her mother's hand. Her mother shifts her grip, and laces her fingers between Linda's.

'I know, Mum,' says Linda, answering the words that she knows are on her mother's lips: we've been so worried.

'We've been driving all night,' whispers her mother.

Linda releases her hand from her mother's grip, and goes back into the living room. Her parents follow her.

'Have you been sleeping here in front of the fireplace?'

'Yes, as you can see,' says Linda, giving a shrug and bending down to pick up the duvet from the floor. She folds it neatly and hangs it on the back of the sofa.

'And you made a fire. That's my girl,' says her father.

Linda goes over to the kitchenette. She takes the tin of coffee out of the cupboard, puts the filter in the coffee machine and measures out the water.

Her mother immediately goes to help.

'Ellen . . .' says Linda's dad, holding her mum back.

'I've got some cake,' says Linda, unwrapping the rest of the lemon sponge that Olga had insisted she take. Linda's parents sit at the kitchen table as though they were guests.

'I'm sorry I went off like that, but I can explain,' says Linda, wanting to get in there before her parents.

'I see,' says her mum, fiddling with the mug she's been given. 'Do you think I could have green tea instead of coffee?'

'Sure,' says Linda. She takes down the tin of tea, fills a saucepan with water and puts it on the hob.

'As you've probably guessed, you're going to be a big sister,' says Linda's father suddenly.

Linda turns towards her parents.

'Why couldn't you admit that before?'

'We've been unlucky twice before, so we didn't want to say anything until we were sure.'

'And now you're sure?'

She turns away, pretending to be busy with the coffee.

'Well, it's been over three months now. And we've even been to an early ultrasound, and had extra tests. Everything seems to be normal and fine. And, not that it matters, but it's a boy. A little brother,' says her mother.

'That's brilliant,' says Linda, smiling.

The news is better than good, since they've had everything checked. This time there really is going to be a baby.

'Aren't you pleased? Would you have preferred a little sister?' asks her father.

'No, no. A brother is perfect.'

The coffee is ready, and Linda pours some out for her father.

'Thanks,' he says taking a gulp. 'That's lovely!'

'You've grown up so much!' says her mother.

'Thanks. I think I have too,' says Linda, unable to hide a smile.

She hears the water boiling in the pan, and takes it off the heat.

'But you do know how frightened we've been?' says her mother, pushing her mug over to Linda. Linda pours the water on a tea bag, wondering what to say. It suddenly feels unnecessary for her to have run off. It's so good that they're here, and that they've driven through the night to find her. All their worrying, right down to the little things, like whether she's dried her hair before going out in the cold; it all points to the fact they love her. Linda knows that. And when she looks into her parents' faces, she feels it even more. She means the world to them. Even with a little brother on the way, she is irreplaceable. They've come all the way here to tell her that.

'Yes, I do know,' answers Linda. 'But I had to go. There's something I've got to put right.'

'What?' asks her mother, leaning across the table. 'Is there something we can help you with?'

'No. I've got to sort this out on my own.'

'But maybe you can tell us what it is? Maybe we can help you with some advice,' suggests her father. 'We were young once, you know,' he says with a smile.

'It's Axel. We fell out this the summer. It was just a stupid misunderstanding. But it was mainly my fault. So I'm the one who needs to apologize,' explains Linda.

'And you couldn't just ring him?' asks her mother, with a little tinge of sarcasm.

'I need to do this,' says Linda. 'Afterwards I'll come home. I promise.'

Her mother shakes her head despairingly, but eventually nods. Her father asks if she can't turn her mobile on at least, and carry it with her. When she tells them she's been stupid and thrown her phone away, her mother simply pushes her own across the table. Linda picks it up, weighs it in her hand, wondering if she should say more.

'I love you both, and the baby too, even if I haven't actually met him,' she says.

'And we love you too, our little treasure,' says her mother. 'But go on now. Do what you have to do.'

'Thank you,' says Linda, putting the phone in her pocket.

It's a cold and clear morning outside. Linda takes the bicycle out of the shed. She feels strong as she peddles up the hill to the main road. It is still very early and she cycles slowly. She focuses on her breathing the way Zak taught her on the train. She lets her mind move gently with her breath. As she breathes in she pushes her left foot down on the peddle. And as she breathes out, she pushes down with the right. And so she rides along, not rushing the day. She'll get there when she gets there.

Chapter 50

Linda leans her bike against the fence, releases her rucksack from the rack, and takes a slip of paper from the side pocket. She has a faint feeling that she has been followed. She turns quickly and looks down the road. Surely it's not her parents again? She has to smile when she sees who her pursuer is. It's just the cat. The one that stayed with her all night. She stuffs the slip of paper in her pocket, and bends down to stroke it.

'How did you get here? I thought you'd left me when you weren't there this morning. Ah, you're such a beautiful pussycat.'

The cat purrs in reply and rubs itself against her legs. Linda crouches down, but then it suddenly reaches out its paw and scratches the back of her hand.

'You're quite right,' says Linda. 'I can't put it off any longer.'

She gets up and looks towards the house. She glances back down at the cat. It grimaces as though it's hissing, but no noise comes out. Linda takes the slip of paper out of her trouser pocket. Her lips move as she reads what's written on it.

Then she walks up to the house. She tries to think about her breathing: breathe in deep and take a step; breathe out slowly and take a step. But it's completely useless. Her breathing is shallow, her heart is thumping, and her hands are so sweaty she's worried the ink on the paper will smudge. Crazy Zak and his stupid breathing exercises, she thinks.

Reaching the top of the front steps, Linda presses the door-bell. No hesitation now! Her ears are pounding. The slip of paper is soggy with sweat. Axel has got to be the one who comes to the door. And he has to come soon. She hears foot-steps in the house. Somebody is walking about in their socks. It must be Axel, since his parents always wear slippers with clunky soles. Those super-healthy clogs from Germany. The door opens. It's Axel.

'Linda?' says Axel, with a questioning look.

He looks paler than he does in the summer, but he's wear-ing the same Brazil football shirt. Yellow doesn't suit him. It doesn't go with his blond hair. Should she tell him? She wants to. She'd rather anything but what she's written on the slip of paper. Still, she clears her throat and looks down at it, her hand shaking:

> *You were the one who taught me the bass,*
> *So I stood on stage and I didn't lose face.*
> *Whenever I dream it's your hands I see,*
> *I need more than friendship, that's now clear to me.*

As Linda gets to the end a shadow comes up behind Axel. A little hand slips into his. A figure with blonde, almost-white hair that hangs loose, and which is quickly pushed to one side with the other hand. Mia.

'Who is it?' asks Mia.

Linda can see that Mia has grown since last summer, and looks even better than she does in her new profile picture. And now Mia rests her cheek against the yellow football shirt, which is also in that profile picture. The dental braces have gone, and so has the puppy fat. And Axel? Have his hands been under that pullover? Has he touched her there? And did he do it with the same sensitive touch as when he brushed Linda's hair from her face last summer?

'It's Linda, as you can see,' answers Axel, releasing his hand from Mia's.

'Linda? I didn't recognize you with your new hair,' says Mia with a giggle, revealing her beautifully straightened teeth.

Linda screws up her slip of paper and flings it away as she jumps down the steps. The gravel crunches under her feet as she runs towards the gate. She puts her hand on the top of the gate and swings herself over. Oh my God, how did I do that? she thinks, landing safely on the other side. Just, whoosh, over the gate, as if it was nothing. She throws herself onto her bicycle and peddles away from Axel's house.

Chapter 51

Linda doesn't stop until she's down by the little shop on the harbour. She throws the bike down, kicks the wheel and flings herself onto a bench that's warming in the sun. Axel and Mia! Of course! That's why he hasn't been on the internet lately, and why the texts have got shorter. Mia! Little Miss Rose-Pink! Little Miss Whatever-You-Say. Or Little Miss I-Don't-Dare, whenever somebody's got a fun idea. Linda imagines Axel asking to touch Mia's boobs, and Mia saying: But of course you can, Axel. Blush blush blush.

'Shit!'

Linda gets up from the bench and kicks the wheel of her bike again. What kind of an idiot is she? Travelling all the way from Trondheim just for this! Everything was meant to be perfect. Eternal, perfect love. She was going to faint – or even die – in his arms. Gazing out at the sea, with the cry of the gulls in the distance. Oh, so romantic! But oh, so ridiculously unrealistic! Why couldn't she have left it as a dream? Why did she have to travel all this way?

It's Zak's fault. And since Zak isn't here to get a

well-deserved kick in the arse, her bike gets a third kick. The bike, which has always been her pride and joy, now has scratches in its metallic blue paint. She turns away from it, and it lies helplessly with its front wheel spinning.

'You're pathetic,' snorts Linda, marching into the shop.

The bell over the door rings brightly, reminding her of the summer. The teenager behind the counter is reading a magazine and barely looks up when Linda comes in. Linda goes straight over to the fridge and takes a Fanta. It's as though she's on autopilot, the same drink she and Axel used to buy and share. Ha! Now she can have a whole bottle of Fanta to herself. She goes to pay. She's got enough money for a little chocolate bar too.

'Wait, don't forget your change,' says the girl behind the counter.

'You can keep it, for luck or something,' says Linda, going back out.

The cat is waiting for her outside. It's rubbing its cheek against the abandoned bicycle, as though marking its territory. It's purring and seems to be in a good mood again.

'You're following me about everywhere. What are you after, eh?' asks Linda, crouching down.

The cat strolls over with its tail straight up and starts rubbing its cheek on her legs.

'Oh, so you think I belong to you, do you?' asks Linda. She laughs, but doesn't stroke it. The scratch on her right hand reminds her that she's dealing with a capricious little creature.

A Fanta is just what she needs now. She puts the top of the bottle on the edge of the bench and knocks off the cap. It clatters on the asphalt and rolls across the uneven surface. The cat leaps about, investigating this new plaything.

Linda is about to put the bottle to her lips when she sees two people peddling towards her on a bicycle. Axel, with Little Miss Rose-Pink on the crossbar, sitting snugly between his arms as he steers, hair fluttering like candyfloss from under the pink woolly hat that matches her pink pullover. She looks like one giant pink sweetie. Linda spits, then on complete impulse, grabs the cat and throws herself behind the corner of the shop. The cat meows loudly and sinks its teeth into her.

'Ow!' she says, dropping the cat, and putting the back of her hand into her mouth. It's bleeding.

The cat looks up at her. Its tail is so bushy, you don't need to be a cat expert to know that it's very angry.

'Don't you understand? We have to hide quietly, you stupid creature,' whispers Linda.

Naturally the cat doesn't answer. The shop bell rings again as Axel and Mia go in. Axel's bicycle is standing neatly parked outside. Linda wants to kick it over. There it stands, newly polished and gleaming in the sun.

'What the hell?' The words just pop out of her mouth as she sees Axel and Mia come out again with a bottle of Fanta, which they are clearly going to share. Linda looks down at the bottle in her own hand, and suddenly doesn't feel thirsty. She doesn't want a whole bottle of Fanta to herself. She slings it onto a heap of dirty snow that hasn't melted away in the sun yet. The contents trickle out. It looks like piss.

Linda hears Mia squealing with laughter. She peeps round the corner, only to see Mia drinking from the bottle as Axel holds it. Oh my God! Can't you even hold your own drink bottle? Then Mia holds the bottle for Axel. A few drops spill and Mia takes off one of her gloves, which are of course also pink, and wipes the drops off his chin. Then she sticks her fingers in her mouth to lick off the orangeade.

I want to puke, thinks Linda. In fact, I think I am going to puke. She goes over to a pile of snow, leans forward and retches, but nothing comes up. She sticks her fingers down her throat, but with the same result. The only thing that lands in the snow is her mother's phone. It has slipped out of her pocket. She's amazed to see that her parents haven't sent her a million texts. Perhaps they've finally realized she's a teenager and can look after herself?

Linda picks up the phone and dries it on her sleeve. Then she gets an idea. *Meet me at our usual place. Important! Linda*, she writes. It's lucky her mother always insisted on storing all her friends' numbers. 'In case of an emergency,' she used to say. Well, this is an emergency! thinks Linda, as she presses the send button.

She walks back and stands by the corner of the shop. She hears Axel's phone go off, and she cautiously peeps around the corner. She sees Axel take his arm from around Mia. He fiddles with his phone, reads the message, and then stuffs it quickly back in his pocket.

'I've got to go,' he says, getting up from the bench.

'Who was it?' asks Mia.

'Er, Mum. I've forgotten to clean the toilet.'

Standing there behind the corner, Linda rolls her eyes to herself. Axel is such a bad liar.

'Okay,' says Mia. 'Shall I come with you?' For once it's a good thing Mia's so thick, Linda thinks to herself.

'To clean the toilet? You want to help me clean the toilet?' says Axel.

'Yes.'

'That's sweet of you, but you really don't have to! I'll ring you later, okay?' says Axel, setting off on his bicycle.

'Can't we at least walk together?'

'It's an emergency, Mum's going crazy,' says Axel, peddling off before there's any more discussion on the matter.

'Bye!' he shouts over his shoulder.

'Bye!' whispers Linda, laughing to herself.

Then she tears the wrapper off the little chocolate bar she bought, stuffs it into her mouth whole and feels instantly better.

Chapter 52

The sun is shining. There are just a few patches of snow left, and there are green shoots lying in wait under last year's yellow grass. But it's still quite cold. It's strange, though, how much earlier the spring seems to arrive down here in the south of Norway. Up in Trondheim there's nothing but snow and frost, followed by rain and slush, then more snow and hail, and then, some time in May, spring arrives for two days, and then – pow – it's summer. Here the spring creeps in from February or March, often bringing endless weeks of rain. A bright, sunny day like this is unusual. Nice, but pretty extraordinary.

Linda puts her rucksack down, and digs out her birthday dress. She gives it a shake, hoping the creases will drop out. She takes off her jacket, and pulls the stunning little black number over her head. Then she puts her jacket back on and keeps her trousers on underneath. Finally she puts on her tiara, before going down to the edge of the water to look at her reflection. The water in the fjord is calm, yet her reflection is unclear. But yes, she looks pretty good. Linda straightens the tiara. Beneath her reflection she sees a crab scurrying sideways to a hiding place under a stone.

She remembers a song that her mum had liked from when she was little. Her mum had sung it so much it eventually got stuck in Linda's brain too. Linda sits on her haunches and peers down at the stone, from which the little crab is poking out. Then she begins singing quietly to herself.

> *Back and forth, we'll row and we'll row,*
> *Off to the place where the fishes all go.*
> *We'll jump in a boat and leave shore behind,*
> *We'll row and we'll row and soon we will find*
> *The world of the fishes far, far below.*
> *Back and forth . . .*

'. . . back and forth . . .' she hears a voice singing behind her, and she sees Axel's reflection in the water. 'Sit here at my side, and off we shall go, in my lovely blue boat . . .' he continues.

He crouches down beside her before saying that he remembers that song too. His school had put on a show in fourth grade, and Axel had been Crusty Crab.

'Well, there's a real Crusty Crab down here,' says Linda, pointing at the crab under the stone.

Axel looks at where she's pointing.

'Yes, a real little devil,' he says.

Linda doesn't answer. She just feels his body close to hers. He is sitting so close. He didn't have to sit so close. Does he like her more than Mia, perhaps? She decides to do it. She turns towards Axel, takes his face in both hands, closes her eyes, and brings her mouth close to his.

'What are you doing?'

Axel leaps up, and Linda topples into the shallow water. Luckily, she saves herself with both hands. But the little crab gets a bit of a shock. It darts out from under the stone and heads for deeper water.

'What are you doing?' Linda yells back, getting up. The skirt of her dress is drenched, and so are the arms of her jacket, feet and all the way up to the knees of her trousers.

'I'm sorry. Did you get wet?' Axel asks.

'As you can see,' says Linda, wringing out her skirt and taking off her jacket and flinging it down on the beach. She can feel water running into her shoes too.

'I'm sorry. You can borrow mine,' says Axel.

He takes off his jacket and gives it to her.

'But won't you be cold?' Linda asks.

'I've got my pullover on,' he says. 'Nice dress, by the way. I hope it's not spoiled.'

Axel picks up Linda's jacket and brushes the sand off it, before tying it round his waist.

'I hope so too. I'm going to be buried in it!' Linda snarls.

'What do you mean?' asks Axel.

Linda doesn't answer. She goes to her rucksack, lying on the sand. She opens it and takes out the brown envelope.

'What's that?'

'You do ask a lot of questions. Open it and see,' says Linda, handing it to him.

Axel opens it and takes out the X-ray. He holds it up to the sun.

'It's beautiful. What is it?'

'It's my heart. You can have it,' says Linda, with a shrug.

'But I . . .' Axel clears his throat before continuing. 'I'm with Mia now. You must have realized?'

'But I'm going to die. I came here because my heart is useless. That picture shows it's completely knackered. The doctor doesn't know why, or how long it'll hold out. I came here because you and I have always belonged together, Axel.'

'What do you mean?'

'That we were destined for each other. From when we were kids. Don't you realize?' Linda says, moving towards him.

Again she tries to kiss him, but he steps back.

'You can't say you're as in love with Mia as you are with me.'

Axel looks at her in reply, bites his lips, and kicks the sand. He takes a deep breath.

'Well, I suppose I was a bit interested in you this summer, but . . .'

'Ha, I knew it,' Linda shouts.

'But you didn't seem to feel the same way. In fact, you were really mean.'

'I'm sorry, Axel. I really am sorry. I handled it badly. When I realized you were interested, something went click in my brain and I turned into a prize idiot! Can't you forgive me? Can't it be the two of us?'

'But I've got a girlfriend, Linda. I like you a lot, but I'm in love with Mia.'

He takes a couple more steps back, as if he wants to be at a safe distance if she tries to kiss him again.

'Mia! Ha! Do you remember how pathetic we thought she was? Like the way she always wears pink, and is so scared of getting any marks on her clothes.'

'You were the one who went on about how pathetic she was. I never said it,' says Axel.

'But you didn't contradict me,' says Linda.

'It's not exactly easy to contradict you, when you get going,' says Axel quietly.

'Are you saying I'm bossy?'

'No, but you can be a bit forceful,' he says without looking at her, concentrating instead on the groove he's making in the damp sand. As if it's really important.

'You're just like all the others,' says Linda.

'Like the others?'

'You're frightened of me, aren't you?'

'No,' says Axel firmly.

'Yes, you are. You're frightened because I'm going to die. That's why you won't kiss me, because you're frightened you might catch some mysterious disease.'

'That's not true. I told you, I've a got a girlfriend. I don't want to hurt Mia. It wouldn't be right,' says Axel, starting to leave.

'Well, what about me, then? I'm the one who's going to die. I'm the one who's come all the way from Trondheim to see you. Just to say sorry, sorry for reading your poems, sorry for laughing at you, sorry I didn't kiss you!'

Axel stops, turns and walks towards Linda. He puts his arms around her and gives her a big hug.

'You are forgiven, Linda. And I hope you'll understand that I can't kiss you. It's just not possible.'

'Why do you have to be so stubborn?' Linda sobs into Axel's chest, sniffing his woolly pullover that smells like sheep.

'You're not bad at being stubborn yourself. To think you've come all the way here, just to say sorry. That means so much to me, Linda.'

'But clearly not enough,' says Linda, pushing him away. 'Piss off,' she says, before heading for the water's edge.

'My jacket?' Axel says hesitantly.

'Do you want me to freeze to death?' Linda snarls.

She doesn't dare to turn around, because her face is covered with tears, and she doubts she looks very tough.

Chapter 53

Linda cycles away from the beach with Axel's jacket over her dress. She feels pretty aimless now, and can't bear to go back to the cottage where her parents will be waiting. Going round a corner, Linda almost cycles into a pink creature-thing. She slams on the brake.

'Hi,' she says, putting her feet on the ground.

'Hi,' says Mia, pushing her hair to the side.

They stand in silence. Linda purses her lips, enjoying Mia's discomfort. The pink troll is clearly feeling nervous now!

'Your hair's really cool. I didn't recognize you earlier,' says Mia.

'I've talked to Axel. He's dumping you.'

'What do you mean? He just went home to clean the lavatory.'

Linda laughs inside. The lavatory indeed! Why can't she say toilet, like anybody else?

'He was lying. We met down on the beach. He kissed me, and he said he wasn't in love with you. He said you were just a way to fill time.'

'I don't believe you,' says Mia.

She tries to walk on, but Linda grabs hold of her so she can't move.

'Ow! Let me go,' Mia squeals.

'Ow! Ow! Ow! Let me go!' says Linda, mimicking her. 'Look, Mia! Can't you see I'm wearing his jacket? Why would I wear his jacket if he wasn't my boyfriend?'

'I don't know,' says Mia, with tears in her voice.

'I don't know,' says Linda, mimicking her again. 'Oh . . . and he's a very good kisser.'

Linda licks her lips demonstratively.

'He tastes of Fanta,' she adds.

Mia is in real floods of tears now, so Linda lets her go. Let her run away like some pathetic newborn calf. Linda has run away from Mia countless times, run away together with Axel, with Mia calling after them. Please wait for me! I can't run that fast!

Linda stands and watches Mia go, and it feels as though a thousand knives were stabbing her in the stomach. She remembers what Zak said when they were on their way up the tower of the cathedral, to see the full moon. That we have an inner compass that tells us right from wrong. That when we do right it feels good, and when we do wrong it feels bad. Yes, Linda knows what these knives in her stomach are telling her. She waits until Mia has gone round the corner, then she flings her bicycle into a ditch, rips off the tiara, and throws that in with it.

'Shit! Shit! Shit!' she shouts.

How can she go to her death peacefully if she carries on

messing things up all the time? She needs to ask Axel's forgiveness again, before she hurts anyone else. Mia might not be her favourite person, but still.

Why is she such a horrible person? Is that why she's got to die? Has God decided she's too evil for this world? Does he have to get rid of her before she turns into Hitler II and exterminates anyone who wears pink? Linda flings herself down at the roadside.

'Argh!' she growls, landing on her back with her rucksack still on. She doesn't remove it – she deserves to be uncomfortable. In fact, she may as well just die there, that would suit her fine. To die and rot in a roadside ditch. She sees the newspaper headlines. LONELY DEATH. GIRL FOUND DEAD IN A DITCH AFTER THREE YEARS. Linda thinks about the girl she read about in the newspaper. The one who died after her first kiss – not in the guy's arms but afterwards, on the sofa. Not quite perfect, but good enough to get in the papers. She wishes again for something like that to happen to her. She and Axel; melting together in a kiss on the beach, and then bang. A romantic story like that would go round the world. Authors would write novels about it, and it might even be made into a movie. But now it seems more likely that she'll go with a little piff, abandoned in a ditch. That was that life. Over and out.

'I'm ready, come and fetch me, do, I'm wearing my pretty dress only for you.' She must have stolen it from a pop song, seeing as it rhymes, but she can't remember which.

And, appropriately, Linda feels a shadow pass over her.

'So you're ready? At last?'

Linda lifts her head and opens her eyes. It's Zak. He bends down and strokes her cheek, brushing off a brown autumn leaf from last year.

'Where have you been?'

As usual he ignores Linda's question, and answers it with another.

'How was the kiss?'

'There wasn't one,' she says moodily.

'Did you change you mind?'

'No. Axel's got a girlfriend.'

'And you're upset?'

'I just don't understand. We were always together. Axel and me. A bit like the story Olga told us about Karl, her husband. They'd been together ever since they were kids. And their love was so strong that it didn't even die after he passed away. That's how it is between Axel and me. Or should be,' sighs Linda.

She picks up her tiara from the ditch. One of the blue stones has fallen off. It's hardly surprising, since it's nothing but fake. Just like love, she thinks, feeling a lump in her throat. Yes, she's certainly feeling sorry for herself.

'It seems that somewhere along the way, you forgot to ask the most important person if that was what they really wanted,' says Zak.

He takes the tiara gently out of her hands. Then he rummages about in the leaves, finds the blue stone and fixes it back in place.

'Who? Axel?'

'No, you,' says Zak, placing the tiara on her head.

'What? Me? Of course that's what I wanted. I wanted it so much I ran away from home and came all the way here. Just to see him one last time and to say sorry, so as . . .'

'. . . to have a romantic end?'

'Yes,' Linda admits. 'But is it so wrong to want that?'

She can feel her cheeks burning.

'But are you sure this is the end?'

'Yes, and now I'm going to die and rot here in a ditch. So just go ahead and strangle me or something. You failed yesterday, when you tried to drown me.'

Linda throws herself down on the grass again, and shuts her eyes. But the sun is shining so brightly, it isn't exactly pitch dark there behind her eyelids.

'Shall I tell you a secret?' whispers Zak.

Linda can feel him stroking her cheek with a blade of grass or something. She doesn't open her eyes to check. She just lets him stroke her calmly. And again everything seems to flow with her breath. And suddenly it's as if there is no division between her body and the ground beneath her; the leaves, the gravel, the withered grass.

'Okay.'

'You promise not to tell anyone?'

'I shall take your secret to my grave,' she says. 'And that isn't far away,' she adds with a bitter laugh.

'You have all the love you need inside you. It isn't true that if Axel doesn't want you, that's the end of love. He's just the person you love, not love itself. Love is much bigger than that. And you have enough love inside you, to love not just Axel but the whole world.'

'Oh, what rubbish! That sounds like something you've read in a positive-thinking book,' says Linda, propping herself up on one elbow. 'I hate the whole world! I'm a vile person! And I'm glad I'm going to die soon!' she says, throwing herself back into the ditch.

A sharp rock catches her back, and she lets out a loud scream.

'Come on, now,' says Zak, taking her hand again and trying to pull her up from the side of the road.

'No!' she says, making herself heavy.

'Yes!' he says, dragging her up with superhuman strength.

'What now?'

'I'll give you a romantic end!' says Zak.

He lifts up the bicycle, sits on the seat, and motions to Linda to sit on the luggage rack.

'Where are we going?'

'No more questions, now, my little emo-princess. Just hop on,' says Zak, laughing.

Chapter 54

Zak takes Linda back to the beach. She is still astonished at how far the spring has come here in the south, at how the landscape is so lush it could be April, and at how brightly the sun is shining, despite the fact that it can rain here for a hundred days at a stretch. She feels Zak take her hand.

'You're not so cold any more,' she says.

'It's you – you've grown accustomed to it,' he says.

He leads Linda back to the place where she'd peered into the water and sang the children's song, before Axel had come and nothing had turned out as she'd planned.

'Do you want another chance?' he asks.

'What do you mean?'

'Yes or no.'

'Yes,' she says.

Her body offers no resistance as he forces her to kneel beside the water. She looks down and sees her own reflection, but not Zak's. She turns. He has gone. Then she hears someone shouting her name.

'Linda! Linda!'

It's Axel. He's wearing the same knitted pullover as before, and has her jacket tied round his waist. She gets up and waits for him to come over. Something rubs itself against her leg. Linda looks down and sees that it's the black cat again.

'You're following me around like some sort of ill omen,' Linda says to the cat, which instantly stops rubbing itself against her and stares up at her crossly, before sauntering off with its tail in the air.

'Linda,' says Axel.

He is out breath, and Linda can see sweat on his temples.

'I've changed my mind. I can kiss you, if you really want,' he says.

'I've changed my mind too,' says Linda.

'Don't you want me to? But you said that you'd come all the way from Trondheim just for that,' says Axel, opening his arms to her.

'Perhaps I came here to find out that I wouldn't kiss you after all,' Linda answers.

'I've always been in love with you, Linda. But you're so cool. And I didn't think you could like anyone like me,' says Axel.

'But you're cool too, Axel. That's why I like you. I like you a lot, which is why I've always wanted to fall in love with you. You're so wonderful. And you're going to kiss a lot of girls. Minus me.'

'I'll always be your friend,' says Axel.

'And I'll be yours,' says Linda, taking off Axel's jacket and handing it to him.

'Thanks,' says Axel.

He unties the sleeves of Linda's jacket around his waist.

'It's almost dry,' he says, holding it out to her.

'Great,' says Linda, feeling for the armhole to put it back on.

'Is it true you're going to die?'

'Yes, it looks as though it'll be a bit sooner than I'd thought,' she says, trying to sound tough.

'It's not fair,' says Axel.

'Perhaps, but I think you ought to go and find Mia now. I did something stupid. I told her that you were going to dump her, and that you and I kissed, and that you were actually in love with me and not her.'

'You did? You're mad,' says Axel, shaking his head.

'That's why you like me,' she answers.

'But then we may as well kiss anyway. You owe me that much!' says Axel.

'Okay, just a little one,' says Linda, giving him a peck on the cheek. 'For eternal friendship.'

'Eternal friendship,' he says, planting a shy kiss on Linda's cheek.

'You'd better go now, before I start to cry or something,' Linda says, covering her face with her hand.

'Because you do love me a bit?' says Axel, trying to catch her eye in the gaps between her fingers.

'What do you think?'

Axel doesn't answer, but he smiles as he pulls his jacket zip up and goes.

'Axel!'

He turns.

'Promise me one thing,' she shouts.

'Anything.'

'You must never stop writing!'

'Never! One day I'll write a whole book about you!'

'Will it have a happy ending?'

'We'll have to see,' he says, smiling.

'See you!'

'I'll miss you!'

Axel waves before he turns again and goes. Linda watches the red jacket grow smaller and smaller until he disappears behind a ridge of sand. And again she feels something rubbing against her leg.

'Are you back again, you stupid freak cat?' she says, without taking her eyes from the place where Axel disappeared.

'Stupid cat, indeed! Now you're being really cheeky!'

And without turning, Linda knows it's Zak.

Chapter 55

So Zak has been there all the time. Linda watches him. His eyes are the last thing to transform, from the golden yellow of a cat's eyes to their more human light blue. She's surprised that she's neither frightened nor shocked.

'Well, aren't you going to say anything?' asks Zak. 'You're usually so full of questions.'

'I'm dead, aren't I?' says Linda, surprised again at how calm she is.

'Yes. But it's not that simple.'

'I thought as much.'

Linda sits down on the beach and burrows her fingers in the sand. She feels how warm the sand is on the surface, where the sun has touched it, and how cool it is a little deeper. Everything feels so intensely real, she thinks. How can it all feel so real?

'You have left your physical body. But as you've probably realized, nothing ever disappears. Including the soul.'

'But when did it happen? I mean, when did I die?' asks Linda hesitantly.

'When do you think?'

'I don't know. The first time I saw you, perhaps? On the tram?'

'No. And that was my fault. I apologize. You should have died *then*, but that's when I started to mess things up,' he says with a sigh.

'What do you mean? Are you Death?'

Zak sighs again. He gets up, brushes the back of his trousers and then walks down to the edge of the sea. He stands there for a moment, his coat flapping in the breeze. Linda says nothing, just watches him, and waits. If he's not Death, then perhaps he is an angel after all? Perhaps God sent him on a mission to fetch her, and then things went slightly wrong. Zak turns to her again.

'I'm just a meeting-soul,' says Zak.

He walks back to where Linda is sitting in the sand. He crouches down in front of her and stretches his right hand out to her.

'I am your little brother,' he says.

Linda drops back onto the sand. She doesn't understand. How can he possibly be her new little brother when he is older than her? How can he be both here *and* inside her mother's stomach? Surely a baby must already have its soul, before being born?

'You'll have to explain,' says Linda, sitting up again.

'Well, firstly it's common to be met by someone you know and love at the moment of death – or more precisely, at the moment of transformation. It usually makes the transition easier. Especially if the person who's dying is a bit scared.'

'But I didn't love you! I didn't even know about you!' protests Linda.

'No, but I knew about you. I knew you would die before I was born, and so I wanted to meet you,' says Zak.

'But does that mean that a baby doesn't get its soul until it's born?'

'No, it just means that before being born, a baby's soul is still able to move freely between the physical and non-physical worlds. When we're born, we begin to forget how it feels to be just a soul without a body.'

'Okay, so you're my little brother and you came to meet me on the tram. But what happened then?'

'I didn't want you to die,' says Zak. 'So I did something that should never be done. I stopped you in the moment of transition. I interfered with the course of events and messed the end up for you.'

'I see,' Linda says, although she doesn't really understand.

'I just wanted to get to know you. I wanted to spend time with you. Do you understand?'

Linda is still very confused, but she nods anyway, mostly because it's nice that Zak wanted to know her.

'So when did I actually die?'

'In the swimming pool, after your second dive. The white light you experienced when you were lying at the side of the pool was the transition. You just didn't realize it. So you were stuck on earth, in a way. And that was my fault,' says Zak. 'If I'd let you die on the tram as planned, you wouldn't have experienced the things that kept you tied to the world. You'd never have found out you were going to be a big sister, or seen the picture of Mia with Axel on your computer, or got together with Oscar. They were all things you had to resolve, which is why your soul ignored your transition. So I had to stay at your side, until you realized you were dead.'

'So none of this really happened?'

'No, not really.'

'I never got to apologize to Axel.'

'No.'

'Did he mind?'

'Yes, you hurt him a lot.'

'Now you're being a bit too honest.'

'Do you really want me to lie?'

'It would feel more pleasant.'

'Life isn't all that pleasant.'

'Uh-huh, and now that I've realized I'm dead? What now?' Linda runs her fingers through her short blue hair.

'Now we must say goodbye, because you're safely on the other side.'

'But how can you be older than me, when you're really just a foetus?' asks Linda, still not quite able to make sense of it all.

'Because there's no time here. Everything happens in parallel. We can be any age simultaneously.'

'Or any animal?'

'Yes! I thought the cat was a brilliant idea. And I hoped it would make you suspicious that things had changed.'

'But it didn't. Stupid me!' Linda laughs.

'Aren't you angry?' asks Zak, looking at her in surprise.

'There's no point being angry now, is there? But there is one thing you ought to tell me. You said time doesn't exist here. That everything happens in parallel. Does that mean I can know what happened after my dive? Was I in the newspapers? And who was at my funeral? Did Axel come?'

Zak doesn't answer, but smiles.

'Come on, Zak! Please tell me. You owe me that much.'

'I can give you something even better,' he says, taking her hand.

Chapter 56

As though in a dream, the landscape around Linda and Zak transforms.

'Like magic,' says Zak, as Linda realizes they're back in the swimming hall.

They are looking down at Linda's body lying lifeless on the edge of pool. But this time Zak doesn't come and pound his fists into her chest. Instead the ambulance men arrive. They bring a defibrillator and try to start her heart, but they fail to revive her. Eventually they put her lifeless body on a stretcher and drape a blanket over it. Then, just as they're about to pull it right over her face, her mother stops them:

'No!' she protests, tears running down her cheeks. 'She won't be able to breathe if you do that!'

'Ellen, Ellen, she's dead,' says her father, putting his arms round her. He nods to the ambulance men and they cover Linda's face.

'Could we rewind a bit? So I can see that perfect dive?'

'No, we must never see ourselves when we're in a human

body. We'd be tempted to intervene, and that would mess things up.'

Zak squeezes Linda's hand gently, and suddenly the floor under their feet changes to a grey linoleum. When Linda looks up they are in a hospital. Her parents are there together with a doctor in an open white coat.

'Your daughter suffered from a rare heart condition. It caused her heart to just stop,' says the doctor.

'But she was so fit and healthy,' her mother protests.

'Indeed, and nobody could have foreseen it or done anything to prevent it. I'm terribly sorry,' says the doctor, and Linda can see from his expression that he truly means it.

'Did I get in the newspapers?' Linda whispers urgently.

'It's okay to talk normally. They can't hear us.'

Zak gives her hand another squeeze, and suddenly they're in front of a rack of newspapers.

'Wow!' Linda exclaims, seeing herself on the front page of all three newspapers: DEATH DIVE. MYSTERIOUS DEATH AT THE BATHS. TRAGEDY IN TRONDHEIM.

'And you know something? Little by little, people will start talking about the pool being haunted by a ghost.'

'Really?' says Linda. 'Like the monk in the cathedral?'

'Better. They'll say that if you feel a warm breath on your neck when you're on the top diving board, then you'll do the best dive of your life.'

'That's brilliant,' says Linda.

She likes the idea of a bit of her still being on earth, as a power for the good. But now, impatient to see more, she squeezes Zak's hand. This time, a long red carpet appears beneath their feet. Linda looks up. At the front of the church stands a coffin. A completely ordinary white coffin. Surrounding the coffin are flowers. Linda suddenly wants to cry.

'It's okay to cry at funerals,' says Zak, putting his arm round her. 'Especially your own.'

Zak and Linda follow the coffin out of the church, where it's lifted into a black car to be driven to the cemetery.

'Do you fancy flying?' Zak asks, and before she can answer, he has whisked her up from the ground and they are floating at a gentle pace above the funeral car carrying her body.

Linda and Zak are the first to arrive at the open grave. Zak puts his hand gently on her shoulder as the coffin and the mourners approach. Everybody from her class is there. Markus and Oscar are walking on either side of Maria. Linda looks around for Axel. Didn't he come to her funeral? As she searches for his face in the crowd, her gaze alights on the hateful Henrik. Henrik is wearing dark glasses, but she can see that even he has tears rolling down his cheeks. Then she catches sight of Axel and, standing beside him, Mia.

'What? Is Mia here?' says Linda.

'Well, you might not believe it, but Mia actually liked you. Even if you did think she was pathetic.'

As the vicar picks up the little spade to scatter earth on the coffin, Linda is quick to squeeze Zak's hand again. There are limits to what she wants to see. Zak laughs a little, and suddenly they have linoleum beneath their feet again. They are standing in front of a door.

'You'll have to go in here alone,' says Zak. 'You'll understand why when you open the door.'

'So, this is goodbye?'

'Let's say *until next time*,' says Zak.

'I'll miss you,' says Linda.

'Time doesn't exist where you are, so you won't miss me. I'm the one who'll miss *you*. I'll miss you all my life, sister.'

'I'll take care of you from this side,' says Linda.

'I know. Go on in now,' he says, nodding towards the door.

Linda stretches her hand out to take the handle. Then, changing her mind, she walks straight through the closed door.

'There are advantages to not having a body,' she says, looking down at herself with quiet satisfaction.

Linda hears a gentle cooing sound. She looks up and sees her mother in a hospital bed. Her face is covered in sweat and she has her hair up in a messy bun. Next to her mother stands her father. They are both peering down at a little blue bundle that's lying at her mother's breast. Linda walks over to her parents and looks down at the little face.

'Isn't he beautiful?' says her mother.

'Yes,' Linda and her father say in chorus.

Linda looks across at her father. But of course he can't hear her. The baby, however, opens his eyes, and Linda instantly recognizes his gaze. It's Zak. It really is him. Her brother.

'Take care of our parents,' whispers Linda.

'Oh, look at those eyes!' exclaims her mother. 'What a wise gaze.'

'Yes, he is the wisest and most amazing baby since Linda was born,' his father replies. 'I wish she could have met him, and that she was here now.'

'You know what,' her mother says. 'I think she is here. It's as if I can feel she's looking after her little brother.'